The Cat of
Yule Cottage

About the author

Lili Hayward is a writer from the south of England with a love for all things hidden, lost and historical. When she isn't writing fiction (or reading it) she can be found wandering bookshops, shouting at weeds on her allotment, or working on various urban growing projects. She lives with her partner in the West Country and keeps the company of two beautiful and opininated ex-stray cats.

LILI HAYWARD

The Cat of Yule Cottage

HODDER

First published in Great Britain in 2016 by
Hodder & Stoughton
An Hachette UK company

1

Copyright © Lili Hayward 2016

The right of Lili Hayward to be identified as the Author
of the Work has been asserted by her in accordance with
the Copyright, Designs and Patents Act 1988.

A CIP catalogue record for this title is available from the British Library

ISBN 978 1 473 64833 3
Ebook ISBN 978 1 473 64834 0

Typeset by Hewer Text UK Ltd, Edinburgh
Printed and bound by Clays Ltd, St Ives plc

Hodder & Stoughton policy is to use papers that are natural, renewable
and recyclable products and made from wood grown in sustainable
forests. The logging and manufacturing processes are expected to
conform to the environmental regulations of the country of origin.

Hodder & Stoughton Ltd
Carmelite House
50 Victoria Embankment
London EC4Y 0DZ

www.hodder.co.uk

'For every family had one cat at least in the bag.'

Christopher Smart, 'For I will consider my Cat Jeoffry'
from *Jubilate Agno*

The house is called Enysyule.

Enysyule. The word lingers on my lips like honey from a spoon. Enysyule: grey and green. Old stone. Old trees. Thatch ochre with lichen. A tiny meadow of waist-high grass, full of sunlight, and a stream running past, a thread of fresh water flowing all the way to the sea. The house stands alone, the only dwelling in the deepest part of a deep valley. Nestled like something precious in the crook of an arm.

I crunch down the cobbled path towards it, the stones broken by time. Overhead, trees arch to meet each other. Their clothes of leaves are growing sparse and threadbare, but they still dapple the light on the ground. It's strange, to walk into silence with only a bag on my back and suitcase in my hand, a layer of country dust replacing the city grime on the soles of my shoes.

The path leads to the front step. I stop there, listening to the scattered birdsong. Minutes or seconds could pass: they don't seem to exist here, only seasons and centuries, measured in saplings and fallen trees. Even the key is old. It's heavy and solid, polished by countless pockets. Finally I fit it in the lock, turn it with a low *thunk*. On the other side a different life is waiting.

I take a deep breath, and push open the door.

It swings into darkness, scraping to a halt. Air, undisturbed for months, floods out, engulfing me. I close my eyes and breathe it in. Worn stone and cold ash, the ghost of baking bread, the sweetness of wooden beams. And something else, something I can't name; a scent of spice and green branches and snow, no sooner recognised than gone . . .

I let my eyes adjust. A long, low room stretches before me, one end disappearing into a huge fireplace, as wide as a creature's maw. Tattered rugs cover the flagstones; an armchair sags in one corner, its fabric ripped to shreds. There's not much furniture, just a long table, a dark dresser, a stool on its side. The initial scent of the house fades, replaced by other, less welcome smells. Dust and damp. Mould and mildew, rot and rust. There's no movement inside. I peer around the front of the cottage, down into the meadow. Nothing. Just a shallow bowl by the doorstep, filled with stagnant green water.

I let my bag fall to the ground with a thud.

What have I done?

*   *   *

In the shadows beneath the ancient holly trees, something stirs. A pair of eyes blink into being. They are yellow as tallow, yellow as corn. They are old eyes, wild as a hawk's, and now they turn towards the cottage.

*   *   *

I scuff my foot along the floor. Dust rises into the air, swirling in the light. A closer inspection hasn't improved matters. The plaster walls are crumbling and smoke-stained. The flagstones are cracked. Several of the diamond-shaped window-panes, so idyllic in the photograph, are broken and stuffed with rags.

This is the old man's fault. If he hadn't been at the letting agent's office, if he hadn't goaded me . . . I had only wanted to see this place, look at it, just once. I thought that might have been enough. I hadn't anticipated a confrontation with a furious local, fuming that his aunt's cottage was being put up for rent. Roscarrow was his name. Mr Roscarrow. He had a face like a seed potato.

'Even if the old bird didn't leave the place to me,' he'd raged, *'even if she didn't, I won't have city people waltzing in here, destroying everything that's precious, squatting in our past and leaving it empty for elevenmonth. Not with Enysyule—'*

The agent had tried to fight my corner. Perhaps she felt embarrassed that I'd come all the way from London to be harangued by an old man. She told him that it wasn't going to be rented as a holiday home, that it was a condition of his aunt's Will that the place be leased as a permanent dwelling, but that didn't pacify him.

'Scavel-an-gow,' he'd sneered at me. *'She couldn't live there! I know that place. She wouldn't even last a night.'*

And so, I snapped. Before I knew it I was telling the letting agent that I'd take the place. I thought the old man would counter my offer with a better one; never dreamed that he was only bluffing, trying to cause trouble. By the time the letting agent mumbled something about the 'caveats' and 'requirements' of the property, I was so surprised I just nodded in agreement. Then she was handing me a pen, shaking my hand, and just like that . . . I became the tenant of a cottage. I look up at the stained ceiling, at the grimy windows, at the valley through the open door, growing cold with evening. I became the tenant of *this* cottage.

With a groan, I lever myself up from the sagging armchair and begin an inventory of the ground floor. The advert said the cottage was supplied 'furnished' but apart from a new mattress and a bottle of gas for the cooker, that just seems to mean it's never been cleared out. There are still books on the shelves, pictures hanging from the walls. The biggest item of furniture by far is the kitchen table. It's huge and weathered, scarred by time. My hand lingers over a deep gouge on its surface. How many dinners have been eaten here? How many bolts of fabric cut, letters written, grazed knees nursed?

Apparently, if the letting agent is to be believed, I will be the first stranger to ever live in this cottage. In its five-hundred-year history, it's only ever belonged to two families. And now, here I am, a starry-eyed writer from the city who has never so much as looked after a garden, let alone an entire valley.

I make my way into what looks like a scullery. Jars and tins remain standing on the shelves. Almost all of them are fish of some kind: pilchards, tuna, sardines. At the back are a couple of bottles of something dark and sticky. I turn one of them around. *Blackberry Wine*, it says, in shaky handwriting, and a date from two years ago.

I set it back down, all at once feeling very alone in this deep valley, with only a few traces of an old woman's life for company. I wish I could talk to someone, just for a minute, but there's no phone service here, and even if there was, who would I call? My mother, my sister? They think I'm mad already for moving so far away, and worse, I've lied to them about the house. I told them that I viewed it before I signed. I waxed lyrical about its fireplace and its garden, the beautiful thatch and the deep green peacefulness, where I'll be able to get *so much writing done*. If they knew I'd signed a year's lease based on one, grainy photograph; if they knew about the unusual conditions of the agreement . . . It doesn't bear think-ing about.

The taps over the scullery sink are corroded at the edges, falling apart, like everything else. I turn them idly. For a few seconds the pipes are silent. Then there's a deep gurgling and water explodes from the end in staccato bursts. It's brown and gritty, but after a while it steadies, clears. I put my hands under the icy flow.

A smeared window looks over the garden, across the pocket-sized meadow and into the woods beyond. I bend my head, splashing cold water onto my tired eyes. As I blink them clear, I could swear that a shadow moves at the edge of my vision. When I look again, there's nothing there. *Just a bird*, I tell myself, even though the back of my neck prickles with the thought that out there, someone – or something – might be watching.

*   *   *

Feet lighter than falling snow move around the cottage, into the brambles that grow thick beside it. The thorns do not scratch, nor do the last fruits, heavy as night, stain the coat that passes beneath them. The meadow grass cools. The bats stir. Darkness isn't far.

*   *   *

I let the cloth fall, staring around hopelessly in the dying light. I've barely even made a dent. I knew the rent was probably cheap for a reason, but I didn't think 'let as seen' would mean *this*.

Dust is thick upon every surface; dead flies and wasps crowd the sills and fall like confetti from the curtains when I shake them. The cleaning supplies I brought with me seem pathetic; a bottle of washing-up liquid, a sponge, some kitchen towels. What did I think I would achieve with them? *You didn't think at all*, a voice at the back of my mind tells me, *you dreamed it would be perfect.*

Doggedly I move towards the huge, dark dresser that lurks in a corner. At least cleaning is better than standing still, letting my imagination run away with me. I swipe the duster over the shelves, the books that lean there. Most of them are leather-bound, warped by time. Their familiar titles make me feel better, like discovering old friends, even far away from home. I brush the dust from a few Dickens and Hardy novels, a bible that's falling all to pieces, a fraying almanac or two. A thin, plain-spined book tempts me to lift it out, to open the cover. It looks like a sketchpad, an inked signature gracing the front page:

Thomasina Roscarrow.

Movement flashes near the open door and I almost drop the book. Fluttering wings, dark shapes. I creep closer to see. Outside, night has started to fall and bats are dipping and weaving against a sky that is purple-grey as dove feathers. Their tiny squeaks make me smile. I go back inside, searching for the light switch. There's one by the door, clunky and old-fashioned. I flip it. Nothing happens. I flip it again, wiggle it up and down. Not even a spark.

Worry bubbling in my stomach, I dig through my bag, searching for my phone charger. Against the wall there's a socket. It looks like something from the 1970s, but I jam the charger in and flick it on, hoping, hoping.

NO SERVICE, the phone tells me. And no electricity. This can't be happening. *Think*, I tell myself sternly; *there must be a fuse box somewhere*. The light is nearly gone, shadows pouring into the cottage like water into a rock pool. Finally I locate the fuse box in the scullery. A spider falls from the brittle plastic casing, and for once I'm too nervous to care, just shake it off and shove the reset switch.

It clunks uselessly.

Panic begins to fill my body, all the emotion of the past few months rushing up to ambush me. I have an emergency number for the letting agent, but no signal. I don't have a car to get to the village. Even if I was certain of which way to walk – and I'm not – I don't have a torch, and the night here is dark. Not the street-lit city darkness I'm used to; thick, country darkness that is quick with living things, that could swallow a person whole.

Get a grip. Light the fire. Find some candles. Light will make everything better. My hands are shaking as I pull open the cupboards and drawers of the scullery, rifling through sticky cutlery and grime-spotted plates. No candles. I trip up the stairs and into the main bedroom, scarcely able to see where I'm going. A huge, dark bed stands bare, a blanket hanging limp on the wall beside it. There's a trunk at the foot of the bed, but it's locked.

I force open the door of the second bedroom. It's a junk room, a few boxes, a broken lamp. It's too dark to see clearly now; soon will be too dark to see anything at all. I run down the creaking stairs. The drawers of the dresser stick. I wrestle them free, sending books toppling from the shelves.

My fingers touch paper and plastic, string and glass before they meet something waxy and cool. I almost sob with relief as I pull out a candle. There's a box of matches on the fireplace, and I hold my breath, pray that they'll work. I didn't think to bring any of my own. Stupid, stupid. I snap the first match in haste but the second one flares beautifully, brightly. Soon, a warm, golden glow fills the corner of the room. I hold the candle in my hands, like a talisman, a sacred thing that will protect me from the dark.

I know that place. The old man's voice comes back to me. *She wouldn't even last a night.*

I realise that I am shaking, with cold as well as fear. The door is still open. Swiftly I slam it shut, turn the key. Anything that might be outside can stay there. I *will* get through the night, alone. The old man was wrong about me. I cling to the thought, try to warm myself with indignation.

My first few attempts to make a fire die, drowning in smoke, but at last some kindling catches, then a log, flames licking up its sides. I sink back on my heels in triumph. It is fully dark outside now. I draw the mildewed curtains and for an instant, catch a glimpse of something slinking beyond the glass, shadow on shadow. I add another log to the fire, making it burn fiercer, brighter.

I won't leave the safety of the flames. Not tonight. Instead, I drag the old armchair close to the hearth, unroll my sleeping bag and huddle it around me. I try to read a book, try to lose myself in the soft sounds of burning wood. I try not to hear the creaks and groans of the cottage, or the lonely call of an owl, like a spirit in the darkness.

Eventually I've had enough. I pick up one of the candles. It wavers in my hand, lighting the way to the scullery. Away from the fireplace, the flagstones are cold and damp. I don't look through the window, just grab one of the bottles I saw earlier, and hurry back to my pool of light.

The liquid gleams ruby red when I hold it to the fire. I twist off the screw cap, take a tentative sip. Sweetness floods my mouth. I close my eyes, tasting berry-laden hedgerows, sunlight on the shining curve of fruit. Slowly, I take another drink of the blackberry wine, thinking of the old woman who must have made it. Am I the type of tenant she had in mind when she wrote her Will, or would she be disappointed to find me sitting here? Finally, lulled by the warmth of the fire and the wine, I feel myself slipping into a doze.

It doesn't last long. A noise jolts me awake and I stare into the darkness, listening hard. It's coming from the front door: a scratching, scrabbling of claws on wood, of something trying to get in. Legends and folk tales race through my mind, stories of lost souls, the fae and the devil's dogs, of ghosts condemned to walk the night for eternity . . . I'm too frightened to open the door to look, too frightened to do anything except pull the sleeping bag over my head, block my ears and wait for it to stop.

I must fall asleep like that, huddled beneath my sleeping bag like a child, because I dream. Not a dream of places or people; a dream of a song. It fills my mind, gradual as dusk, deep as ore buried beneath the earth. There are no words I can repeat, no tune I can hum. Yet somehow I know what it means.

It's a song that starts with winter. I hear the whisper of snow, the snickering of frost as it creeps across the ground. I hear grass snapping underfoot, the groan of the water, frozen in a stream. I feel my blood running slower, ice forming in my veins, and just as I think I will freeze to death, there is a shift. The cold recedes, and everything melts into spring.

There is a thundering of heartbeats as a thousand newborn things force their way into the world. I hear darkness stalking them on silent paws, waiting to attack, uncontrollable as the tide. Yet I hear those same paws frisking, leaping into summer to catch at sunbeams. I hear berries and birds and cascades of flowers that perfume the short, breathless nights.

Then, I hear that ripeness bursting, plummeting into autumn. The song slows, deepening into morning mists, into long, dark nights, ebbing towards the end of the year. I hear the leaves parch on the trees, and the blaze of All Hallows; I hear the horns of a hunt, its riders racing across the sky, chasing the old year down. I hear a night of feverish spirit, when order is lost from the world.

The song is reaching its zenith, and I realise that everything I have heard, all of it has been leading to this. The melody drops, like softly falling snow, into the Yuletide. A night where old and new meet in the burning of the hearth, when time is *now* and *was* and *will be* all at once; when bad blood is forgotten and hearts can be changed by a single, whispered word. And I realise that I am crying at the beauty of it, I am reaching towards the singer . . .

I wake, one hand outstretched. I try to remember the song, the melody, but between one breath and another the notes are fraying, falling to pieces. For a moment, the cottage seems filled with the scent of greenery, freshly cut from cold trees. Then that too is gone.

In the darkness outside, a sound rises, and I listen again in hope. But it isn't the song, beautiful beyond words; it's just a cat, yowling to the moon.

★   ★   ★

The song lasts all through the night. It has been sung for a thousand years at the start of every season, will be sung for a thousand more. An old song; always and never the same. It lasts until the sky turns grey, until the birds that have not fled the cold begin their cautious morning greetings. The singer listens. The woman sleeps.

★   ★   ★

I blink my eyes open. Soft light is filtering through the curtains, and from outside I hear birdsong, echoing around the valley. Daylight. I made it. The longest night of my life, but I made it.

Limbs stiff and cramped, I unfold myself from the armchair. The fire is almost dead, just a couple of embers slumbering in thick coats of ash. I'll have to find more wood. I'll also have to brave the outside bathroom. Shivering, I pull on my shoes. All around me is the evidence of my sleepless night; the dresser drawers hanging open, the burned-down candles, the books spilled from the shelves. In the light of day, it all seems rather silly. Still, I can't forget the fear I felt, or the song that filled my dreams.

I open the door. Outside, it's a perfect autumn morning. Mist hangs low through the valley, leaves blaze orange and gold upon the trees. I take a deep breath of the crisp air, hopefulness flooding through me once again. As I step onto the path, something stirs within the branches of a tree, a shadow that is too big to be a bird. I feel eyes watching.

'Come out,' I call, the sound of my voice jarring in the stillness. 'I know you're there.'

Sure enough, there's a flurry of leaves, and a huge dark shape leaps onto the garden path before me. Its fur is black as coal and fluffed out against the chill, sporting a collection of leaves and twigs. In the city I might have gone over, made soft noises and held out a hand to stroke it, but here, I don't.

It wouldn't be right. The cat looks up and for an instant I'm pinned to the spot by a pair of eyes, yellow as tallow, yellow as corn.

'So you're the cat who lives here, are you?' I force myself to ask, wondering why I feel so strange.

The cat yawns nonchalantly, begins to wash a paw.

'I suppose that was you last night,' I carry on, 'scratching at the door, caterwauling for hours on the roof when I was trying to sleep?'

This seems to annoy the cat. It thrashes its tail on the path and looks off in the opposite direction.

'Look, if we're going to live together, we'll have to reach some kind of agreement, OK?' I tell it reasonably. 'No waking me up in the middle of the night, no yowling or scrabbling at the door. If you want to be inside, you'll have to ask me before I go to bed.'

The cat stands up and stalks off into the meadow, tail raised haughtily.

'One day alone,' I mutter, trudging towards the bathroom, 'and I'm already a mad cat woman.'

I do my best to make myself presentable, although – of course – the boiler is broken, so I have to make do with cold water. Mrs Welwyn, the letting agent, invited me for Sunday lunch at the pub when she gave me the key yesterday. To welcome me to the community, she said, evidently with Mr Roscarrow's hostility in mind.

It's a beautiful day for a walk, autumn's colours flaring bright, a breath away from winter. Sitting on the front step of the cottage, I unfold a map. I found it when I was re-stacking the books on the dresser. It's hand-drawn, goodness knows how old, the paper yellowing, backed onto leather that's soft with age. *Enysyule*, it says at the top. I pore over the drawing, shaking my head in disbelief. Fourteen acres of woodland surround the cottage, stretching up the valley's steep sides. I trace a route down the eastern edge towards an arrow that's labelled *Lanford,* pointing the way to the village. Next to it, on the valley's boundary, someone has drawn a circle, written the word *Perranstone.*

I walk to where the path should start, at the edge of the little meadow. Through the wet vegetation I see what looks like a cobble; the remains of a road that must be centuries old. I hesitate. It's almost completely overgrown with grass and nettles. Perhaps I should take the long way round, up the hill and out onto the country lane. I glance over my shoulder, feeling like I'm being watched. The cat must be around somewhere. So far, my efforts to make friends with it have been spurned. I opened one of the tins of tuna from the pantry, emptied the bowl of green, slimy water and re-filled it with fresh, only to be ignored. Later, I caught it eating what looked like a dead moth. A flash of black on the thatched roof catches my eye. The cat is sitting up there, sunning itself, staring down at me in judgement.

Folding the map into my bag, I take a deep breath, and plunge down the path. The bushes are full of insects, and more than once I find myself shuddering and brushing crawling things from my sleeves. After a minute or two, the grasses drop back, and the space becomes clearer. The cobblestones rise up out of the mud and moss, leading the way downhill and into the stream itself. A ford, I realise. I splash through it, trying to imagine what it must have been like here hundreds of years ago.

My feet follow the path of their own accord, even when it disappears beneath tree roots or breaks up, its cobbles scattered. Lost in thought, I don't notice the clearing until I am almost upon it. When I do, I stop dead, the breath catching in my throat.

A stone stands in the centre of a holly grove. The branches here are so thick, they look almost woven together, a near impenetrable wall, save for a single gap on either side. The holly trees must be ancient, nearly thirty feet tall in places, shadows thick between their glossy green leaves. But the stone . . . it looks even older, ravaged by time, moss and lichen draped across it, like a mantle. It's as tall as me, and as wide as my outstretched arms, a round hole pierced through its centre.

My skin tingles all over. What on earth is it? I pull out the map. There, at the valley's edge is the inked circle, the word *Perranstone.* This strange, ancient thing marks the boundary of Enysyule. Trying to ignore the fluttering in my stomach, I step gingerly into the clearing.

Immediately, my head whooshes, as though I've stood up too fast. My vision clouds, my ears ring and for a moment, everything is dark. I hear storm-lashed branches and beating wings, the screaming of a horse and a woman's cry . . .

I blink, and it's gone. The valley is just as it was, distant birdsong, autumn sunlight. I stare hard at the stone, and it's just that; an old, old stone, standing silently in a clearing. Now I can see that the cobbled road re-emerges on the other side, disappearing into the wood. Why didn't Mrs Welwyn mention this to me? It seems important, an ancient monolith in the back garden; if that's what it is. Maybe she thought it didn't matter. Maybe she doesn't even know it's here . . . I wouldn't have known, without the map.

I move around the edge of the clearing, keeping my distance from the stone. The second my feet leave the holly grove – leave the bounds of Enysyule – something changes. It feels like time is welling up around me, bringing the modern world with it. All at once, I can I hear the drone of a plane overhead, catch a waft of fertiliser from a field, hear a dog barking somewhere close by.

Very close, in fact, and getting louder, more frenzied. I look up as the undergrowth explodes in a flurry of leaves and a dog comes pelting towards me, barking its head off. Instinctively, I step back into the clearing.

The dog stops in its tracks. It's some kind of collie, ears perked, muzzle open, brown eyes staring at me intently. It wuffs and lowers itself as if to jump, but changes its mind, half-growling and whimpering, padding back and forth, right where the clearing meets the wood.

'Maggie?' A man's voice echoes through the tree trunks. 'Maggie!'

A figure comes into view. Green jacket, flat cap, gun over the shoulder. I groan inwardly. This looks like trouble. The man stops when he sees me. A dead pheasant hangs in his free hand.

'Can I help you?' he calls. His voice has an upper-class edge.

'I'm just walking to the village,' I call back, feeling my face grow hot. 'Or I was. Your dog seems to have other ideas.'

'Well,' he says, crunching closer over the leaves, 'that's probably because you're trespassing on private land. What are you doing here?'

'I'm not trespassing,' I snap. 'This land happens to be mine. Sort of.'

At that the man laughs, pushing back his hat. He's young, I realise, maybe even younger than me, with messy, dark blond hair, grey eyes and stubble across his chin.

'In that case, I'm sorry.' His smile invites me to join it. 'I thought you were some amateur historian, poking around without permission.'

'No. I live here. As of yesterday.'

His eyes widen. 'So *you're* the infamous Miss Pike!' He shoves the pheasant under his arm and holds out a hand. 'Delighted to meet you. I'm Alexander.'

'I'm—' I automatically take his hand, before his words catch up with me. 'What do you mean "infamous"?'

'Lanford's a small place, Miss Pike. You've caused quite the stir already.'

He releases my hand. Cold air rushes in to take its place.

'I don't see how,' I protest. 'I haven't even met anyone yet.'

'Being a stranger is enough.' He grins. 'Anyway, now you've met me.' He steps back, looks at me closely. I feel very conscious of my hastily combed hair, curling in all directions, my lack of sleep. 'I have to say, you're not at all what I expected.'

'And why's that?' I try not to sound defensive, hunching my hands into my pockets.

'Well, *I* heard you swept into town and all but bribed the letting agency to give you the place, just like that, cold as ice—' He obviously sees the dismay on my face, because he stops, looking apologetic. 'It's just stupid gossip,' he says. 'They'll know it isn't true the second they meet you.'

'I hope so.' I try to muster a smile. 'Actually, I'm on my way to meet some people at the pub now. Or I was . . .' I look pointedly at the dog, busy sniffing around the roots of trees.

The man bellows out a laugh. 'Oh yeah. Sorry. Maggie's not a fan of that big old rock for some reason.' He jerks his chin at the holed stone. 'They say animals know things, right?'

I think of the black cat, staring at me from the roof, yowling all night, the sound merging with my dreams . . .

'I'm not sure I want to believe that,' I murmur.

'Me neither.' Alexander shoulders his gun. 'Shall I point you in the direction of the village? I'm going that way myself.'

For the second time that day, I step across the border of Enysyule.

'So, are you local?' I ask as we walk. The sunlight filters through the trees, leaves falling slowly through the air, like flakes of gold.

'Yup,' the man swings his pheasant. 'Local as they come. My family have been here for donkey's years.'

'Seems like everyone has, except me.' A leaf dances down, brushing my cheek. I catch it, stare at the bright yellow against my skin, darker than Alexander's. 'I didn't really think about that.'

'Don't worry, they'll all warm up eventually. Well, maybe not old Roscarrow, but he's a miserable git. He's always sore about something. Right now it just happens to be the cottage. He'll soon find something else to moan about and stop—' He shuts his mouth quickly.

'Roscarrow,' I frown, 'I know him, he was there at the letting agency. What is he going to stop?'

'Nothing, it's ridiculous, don't worry about it.'

'Tell me, please.'

His cheeks turn a bit pink. 'He's got a wager going with some of the men in the village,' he says, fidgeting with the pheasant's claws. 'About how long you'll last here. He's been trying to think of ways to drive you off.'

For a moment, I'm stunned. I know I shouldn't be surprised, should have anticipated this reaction but . . . anticipating hostility and hearing proof of it are two very different things.

'Miss Pike?' Alexander says. 'Are you OK? I'm sorry. I shouldn't have said anything.'

'I'm fine.' I push down the anger. I'll have to deal with it later. Making friends has suddenly jumped up my list of priorities. 'And stop calling me Miss Pike.' I smile. 'My name's Jess. Well, Jessamine, but only my mum calls me that.'

'Jessamine,' he repeats. 'That's beautiful.'

I catch him looking sideways at me as we walk on.

'So, I'm guessing you've moved here with someone? Boyfriend, partner . . .?'

'Nope.' I hop over a fallen log. 'Just me.'

'Left anyone back in London?'

Ahead of us, Maggie the dog rushes about, yapping at leaves. I pick up a stick to throw.

'My family are there. Apart from that, no. Just someone I'd rather not see again.'

'Oh. Sorry.'

Maggie interrupts, making us laugh by trying to drag a small tree along the path. Ahead, the canopy is thinning out, the path bends and all at once green water is glistening before us. A river, or an estuary, I can't work out which. In the middle of its channel, boats are bobbing, and the noise of an outboard motor works its way towards us, a distinctive *put put put*. Trees grow all the way down to the shore, as though jostling to get a look a their reflections.

'Lanford,' says Alexander, stopping beside me. 'Just follow the river around, and take the bridge over the creek. You'll find the pub in no time. It's called the Lamb.'

I don't reply, trying to take it all in. Somewhere behind us is Enysyule. For the first time, I understand how truly hidden it is; a deep green fold between deep green hills. I look back and of course I can see no sign of it. Instead, I catch a glimpse of sunlight on arched glass windows, the top of a tower, protruding from the trees.

'What's that place?' I ask, pointing.

'Oh, that's the big house,' he says vaguely. 'Listen, what are you doing on Friday?'

'What?' I feel my face grow hot. 'I, um, not much. I mean I have a lot of work to do. So, working, probably.'

'Working? On the house?'

'No, on a book, actually. I'm a writer. I'm supposed to have a new manuscript finished by Christmas so . . .' I trail off pathetically.

'A writer!' He smiles. 'That's cool. I was just asking because it's Halloween. I'm having a bit of a party. Wondered if you wanted to come, meet some more of the locals?'

I feel so stupid. Of *course* that's why he's asking. 'Oh. Right.'

'Hold this,' Alexander thrusts the pheasant at me, and I find myself gripping its scaly legs. A faint smell of blood rises, mingling with the must of dead leaves and cold, green river water. 'Here,' he scribbles on a piece of paper, exchanges it for the pheasant. 'That's my number. Give me a call if you change your mind.'

He's gone before I can answer, whistling for Maggie, striding away into the wood.

'You're here!' a voice booms across the pub. It's crowded and noisy, and dozens of pairs of eyes turn to look when I walk in. I feel myself flush crimson as Michaela Welwyn, the letting agent, comes barrelling towards me.

'Miss Pike.' I'm engulfed in perfume as she kisses me on both cheeks. 'So pleased you came. Did you find your way? How's the house? I'll get you a drink, what will it be? Beer, cider?'

'Yes, thanks,' I manage to say, 'I'll have a—'

'Great.'

Then she's gone, leaving me stranded, an object of curiosity for the pub's customers once more. Someone is waving at me from the back of the room; I recognise Liza, Mrs Welwyn's assistant, and weave my way towards her.

The Lamb is a cosy place, low-ceilinged, full of nooks and deep, cushioned window-seats. The walls are crammed with memorabilia; photographs and paintings, horse brasses and commemorative plates. It smells of woodsmoke and dried hops, roasting meat and beer. I wonder whether it has always smelled this way.

'Good to see you again,' Liza says, shifting a drowsy baby onto her shoulder. 'Did Michaela ambush you at the door?'

'Yes,' I laugh, taking off my coat. 'She's gone to get me a drink, at least I think that's what she said.'

'You'll get used to it,' Liza grins. 'Michaela used to be a house mistress at a boarding school. I don't think it's ever really worn off.'

She introduces me to the others at the table. Her husband Dan, who smiles at me, and their small daughter Daisy, who buries her face in her father's shirt. Michaela's husband Geoff, who nods up from his paper, their friend Julie, cousin Pete . . . I murmur greetings to all of them, trying to remember their names.

'This is Miss Pike,' Liza announces, 'she's renting Enysyule.'

Is it my imagination or does the sound in the pub dip for a second? Michaela's husband looks up at me with renewed interest.

'Please, call me Jess,' I say, taking a seat. The noise swells again, clinking glasses and voices and laughter.

'So, Jess,' Liza looks a bit worried. 'How is the cottage?'

'It's, um, slightly more rustic than I expected,' I admit. 'And the electricity isn't working.'

'Not surprised,' interrupts cousin Pete. 'Can't believe you rented it to her in that state, Liz. Not had a snip of work done to it in what, twenty years, Geoff?'

'Twenty years,' agrees Michaela's husband, going back to his paper.

'Old Miss Roscarrow was a bit doolally,' Pete continues in a stage whisper.

'Oh, she twadden,' Julie dismisses, 'she was just different is all. All the Roscarrows are that way.'

'We thought she was a witch when we were kids,' Dan smiles over Daisy's head. 'Used to dare each other to go down to Enysyule on Allantide. Never had the guts to actually do it, though.'

'Allantide?' I ask, glad to shift the conversation away from me.

'Halloween,' explains Liza, 'and don't go telling her stories of ghosts and witches, she's only just got here.'

'Not just Halloween!' Dan replies in mock-indignation. '*Nos Kalan Gwav*! The first night of winter, where spirits walk the earth and we light our fires, to keep away the darkness that's to come.' He makes a ghostly noise at Daisy, who laughs delightedly.

I smile, at the same time remembering the fear in my belly last night, when I thought I was to be stranded, alone in the darkness, something watching from the shadows. I start to bring up the topic of electricity when Michaela comes back, two brimming pints in her hands.

'Didn't know what you wanted,' she puffs, 'ale or cider. So I got both.'

The next few minutes pass in a frenzy of food ordering and cutlery laying. I take a sip of cider. It's cloudy and tart, reminds me of the apples I used to steal, small and hard as golf balls, from a neighbour's tree as a child. As soon as everything's calm again Michaela leans back in her chair, looks at me seriously over her bright pink glasses.

'So,' she says, 'did you meet the cat?'

They're all looking at me.

'Yes,' I say awkwardly, wondering why they're being so odd. 'Though he doesn't seem very friendly.'

Michaela and Liza exchange a look. 'Well, don't worry about that for now,' Michaela mumbles. 'You'll get used to each other.'

'I suppose we'll have to.' I take another mouthful of cider. 'What do the conditions of the tenancy *actually* say? I mean, I don't mind it being there, but I don't know a thing about looking after cats. I've never had one before. Isn't there a relative or someone who can take—'

'No,' says Pete.

'It's not that—' starts Michaela.

'Always been a cat at Enysyule,' Dan says at the same time. He flushes when everybody turns to stare at him. 'What?' he demands. 'There has!'

'I'm afraid it's just part of the agreement,' says Liza, shooting the rest of them a meaningful glance. 'It was Miss Roscarrow's wish that whoever rents the house must also care for the cat. She was very clear about it.'

Pete snorts. 'She would've left that whole bloody place to the cat if she could. You know she tried to. Like I said, she was completely—' Julie clouts him on the arm. 'Ow!'

'She tried to leave it to a *cat*?' I ask, incredulously.

'It was an ... unorthodox situation,' Michaela admits, looking a bit flustered. 'While it wasn't legal for the cat to inherit, Miss Roscarrow could stipulate that the cottage be rented, rather than sold, so the cat is cared for there, for the duration of his life.'

'And when the cat dies ...?'

Michaela shifts in her chair. 'Then technically the agreement would become null and void. I wouldn't worry about it.'

It seems like something worth worrying about to *me*, though it's too late now, I suppose. And anyway, I've signed the lease for a year.

'What's the cat called?' I ask instead. 'Maybe I'll have more luck making friends if I know its name.'

'Perrin,' they all say at once.

'Perrin,' I repeat, trying not to stare at them.

I can't shake the feeling there's something they're not telling me, but soon the food arrives, and I forget almost everything else. After a night and morning eating only biscuits and apples, I find that I'm starving. Roast beef, covered in thick, shiny gravy, crispy potatoes, carrots that taste like they've been pulled from the ground that very morning.

'They probably have,' laughs Liza, 'they're from your mate's farm, aren't they, Pete?'

'Yep,' Pete spears one with his fork and looks at it mournfully. 'These are the last of them for the year.'

Despite their odd behaviour they're a cheerful lot, and slowly I begin to relax in their company. Dan is a teacher at the primary school, I discover. Julie is a nurse, Michaela's husband runs the local museum and visitors' centre. Pete mumbles something about 'scrap' and heads off to the bar.

'He's a beachcomber,' Michaela tells me out the corner of her mouth. 'Keeps an eye out for storms, knows the best spots for wreckage and washed-up goods.'

'Isn't that illegal?' I can't tell if they're having me on or not.

'Just another fine Cornish tradition,' winks Dan.

Pudding arrives, whortleberry crumble, I'm told. I've no idea what a whortleberry is, but it's delicious; dark berries, oozing into the custard. Liza and Dan's daughter Daisy manages to make a spectacular mess of herself.

After a while, they fall into talk about village affairs. I'm happy to sit back, stomach full, and let the conversation wash over me. The pub has emptied out a bit now, and I can see the fireplace at the other end of the room, logs crackling gently in the hearth. It's surrounded by a collection of worn leather armchairs, which are occupied by a collection of equally worn leathery men, talking in a low, soothing rumble. I'm about to look away when I realise that someone from the group is watching me; someone a good forty years younger than the men around him. Strong features, a dark beard. Perhaps it's the second pint of cider making me bold, but I don't look away.

'Who's that?' I ask the table.

The man looks like he has just come in from the outside, a woollen hat pulled down over his hair, cheeks whipped pink by the autumn breeze.

'That's Jack,' Dan says, raising a hand in greeting. The dark-haired man gives an awkward nod back, before finally looking away. 'Jack Roscarr—' Liza's elbow meets his ribs too late.

'Roscarrow?' I ask them. 'As in, old Miss Roscarrow who used to own Enysyule? And the Mr Roscarrow who was so rude to me at your office?'

'I'll just go and change the baby,' Dan mumbles, making his escape.

'Yes,' Liza says reluctantly. 'Jack is Mr Roscarrow's grandson. They work together at the boatyard.'

They're all watching for my reaction. I could let the matter drop. I could shrug it off, could wait for the rest of the village to grow accustomed to me, to get over their curiosity and idle gossip about the new girl in town.

He's got a wager going with some of the men in the village, about how long you'll last here. He's been trying to think of ways to drive you off.

'Excuse me,' I tell the table. Before they can say anything, I stand up and stride over to the old men beside the fire.

'Sorry to interrupt,' I say brightly. 'I was just wondering if Mr Roscarrow here could give a message to his grandfather.' They gape at me in astonishment. The dark-haired man says nothing, only looks up at me cautiously. His eyes are striking – bright hazel – and I feel my resolve falter, but there's no going back now. 'Please tell your grandfather that I know all about his stupid wager,' I say clearly. 'Please also tell him that he's going to be disappointed. I'm not going anywhere.' I take them all in with a glance. 'Thanks so much for your warm welcome.'

I feel my face threatening to turn red as I walk back to the table, my insides fizzing with nerves.

'Bravo,' laughs Pete, 'you tell 'em.'

'I'm sorry, Jess,' Liza says quietly, 'we didn't want to upset you.'

'It's OK.' I pick up my pint and drain it to the dregs.

Michaela makes a disgruntled noise in her chest as she shrugs into her coat. 'I'll be having words with Mel Roscarrow.'

'We'll have to talk to him anyway, if the electricity at the cottage isn't working.' Liza winces. 'He's actually your closest neighbour,' she explains. 'The substation is on his land.'

'We'll go and set him to rights.' Michaela thumps my shoulder. 'You'll be all right without leccy, for another day or two?'

As we walk towards the door I see Jack Roscarrow, watching me from his seat by the hearth.

'Of course,' I tell her, loud enough for him to hear. 'I'll be absolutely fine.'

The walk back to Enysyule feels colder, despite the warmth of the food and the cider in my belly. The day is waning, the sky turning the colour of pearl, the air hazy with smoke from the village's fireplaces. I stick to what looks like a path through the wood, hoping it's the same one I walked with Alexander. I wasn't paying much attention at the time.

It's funny, this morning I couldn't wait for a dose of civilisation, for voices and people and cars and phone reception, yet now ... I want to plunge back into the green stillness, light my own fire, dream beside the hearth and begin the long, gradual process of making the cottage my own.

Once again, the Perranstone looms out of the gathering dusk before I expect it to. I linger, one foot in the present, one foot on the valley's boundary, where time doesn't flow, but pools, the past welling up into the present ... I step forward and leave the world behind me.

The stone's surface seems to shift in the half-light, pale, glimmering. It draws me in; I want to lay my hands upon its surface, want to bend and peer through the hole in its centre and see more than reality on the other side. I don't. Not yet. Besides, there's the cottage to open, logs to bring in, if I don't want to spend the night shivering in the darkness. I stand at the bottom of the meadow to look up at the cottage, waiting quietly in the falling evening. I can't believe that it's my home.

'Good evening,' I whisper to it, to the whole valley.

In response, there's a rustle of leaves, a slink of shadow and the cat pads out of the brambles. Its eyes glow in the twilight.

'Hello again,' I say, walking up the path towards it. 'I've been hearing about you. Your name is Perrin. Mine is Jessamine.'

The cat settles down on the front step, like a host awaiting a visitor. After a moment, it lets out a *meow*. I grin. Progress.

'Here,' I tell it, rummaging through my bag. 'I brought you some dinner.'

Wrapped in a napkin are a few pieces of fish that Liza and Dan's toddler didn't finish. I lay them on the ground. The cat gives me a hard look, then goes to sniff the food suspiciously. I get on with unlocking the cottage, searching through the woodshed for logs that aren't green with moss. By the time I stagger back, my arms full, the cat has gone. So has the fish. I step inside with a smile. One point to me.

★   ★   ★

There was a time when every one of these gnarled trees was a sapling. When the stream was almost a river, flowing full and loud as a farm girl's voice raised in song. When there was no house at all; just the water and the stone and the eyes that watched. Then came the cottage, built from moorstones and fieldstones, the road, the people. They first came here on an autumn day, many years ago, never dreaming that their lives would change this place forever.

*   *   *

It is late autumn in the valley and the trees are blazing, their leaves falling like pages torn from a gilded book. The cottage's stone walls are clean from carving, its thatch new and bright. It waits for the people who have come to make their home here: a man and a woman, she with bright hazel eyes and a body heavy with child.

She moves through the meadow, down to the stream, where the path dives beneath the shallow water of the ford. Her face is red and tight with pain, and she digs her fists into her stomach, though it is not the child that ails her.

There is a boulder beside the stream, a way marker, set there long ago for travellers who happened to stray. With difficulty, she stretches her arms around it, like a lover. Her fingers trace the marks of carving on the back – recent carving – made by a fine knife. She begins to cry, feeling the shape there, a promise made in the spring, broken by the time the dog roses faded, leaving her to face a wedding to another, a vow with a secret in her belly, and her only consolation this cottage: a reward for her silence. She knows the child will not belong to the village or the man it will call father. It will belong to this valley, where it was made.

After a time, a voice echoes across the meadow, calling her name. She pushes herself back, scrubs at her face, and looks up, straight into my eyes . . .

I wake abruptly. Everything is dark, the fire a dim red glow. No falling leaves, no woman with eyes of bright hazel. I rub at my forehead, disorientated. There's a noise coming from somewhere. The gurgle of water? A voice calling? No, closer than that. I drag the sleeping bag from my head to listen.

An insistent yowl, then another. The breath I hadn't realised I was holding whistles out of me. It's the cat. Just the cat, wanting to be let in. Its shouting must have woken me. Carefully, I take a candle stub over to the door. It gutters in the rush of cold air, and a shadow slips past my ankles, like dark oil. By the time I have bolted the door and turned around, the cat is already seated in the armchair, nestled in the warmth of my sleeping bag. It looks up at me and makes a chirruping noise as if to say *how thoughtful of you.*

'That's my bed,' I tell it, shivering. 'You'll have to move.'

It circles once and settles down, looking immensely comfortable. Any other cat I would pick up and dump on the floor . . . Tentatively I balance on the very edge of the seat, and start to wedge myself into the tiny space the cat has left. How it's able to take up the entirety of such a large chair is a mystery. Finally, I manage to drag about a quarter of the sleeping bag over me. The cat looks up, squashed and disgruntled about it.

'This how it's going to be, is it?' I ask, from my awkward position.

The cat responds by digging its claws into the sleeping bag and beginning to purr, a low rumbling sound, filling the room like the sound of soft rain.

The next morning I scrub at the windowpanes, trying not to let my thoughts wander, to no avail. In London, people will be huddled in coffee shops or hurrying between offices and tube stations, wrapped in the new season's coats. I try not to think about the people I've left behind there, try not to imagine my ex, moving his stuff around our old flat, wiping out traces of our relationship, stepping around the small pile of boxes that contain my life, and which stand, waiting for the courier. I scrub harder and the newspaper disintegrates in my fingers. I sigh and drop it to the floor.

Yesterday's glorious sunshine has disappeared without a trace. Outside, grey sheets of rain are falling, which means

I'm stuck indoors, no music, no radio, only my thoughts for company. And the cat. I have to admit, his presence makes me feel better, even if he's barely moved from the sleeping bag all day.

'All right for you,' I mutter, climbing down from the windowsill.

At least the downstairs rooms are starting to look respectable. I've cleaned every windowpane that isn't broken, the huge, old table has been scrubbed, and I found a broom to sweep the floor free of ash. Even though the electricity *still* isn't working, I've figured out how to use the gas cooker. I wrap my cardigan around myself, and go to fill the old stove-top kettle. I can't turn on the lights, or charge my phone, or use my laptop, but at least I can make tea.

The sound of bubbling water breaks my dream from last night. I close my eyes, trying to capture it again. The sound of water, gurgling through the ford, a woman with bright hazel eyes and a child in her belly, her arms around a way marker, tracing marks carved into stone.

A shrill whistle snaps me back to the kitchen and I turn off the gas, feeling strange. Across the room, there's a flicker of movement. The cat is staring at me intently. *Overactive imagination*, I tell myself, pouring water into a mug, *this is what happens when you don't write for a while, you start seeing stories everywhere*. I sit down at the table, take out a notebook, and try to find my way back into the world I was writing, before I left London. A world to disappear into, full of journeys and secrets, possibilities and old magic . . .

The back of my neck tingles. Did I see a way marker when I walked through the ford yesterday? I can't remember. It would only take me a minute to check. I try to push it from my mind, try to start work on a new scene, only to find myself writing about a valley, about a man with a knife carving a promise into stone. I push the notebook away, disgusted with myself.

'This is ridiculous,' I tell the cat. It stretches out a paw, makes a low noise of agreement. 'And you're no help.'

Still grumbling, I pull on my boots, sling a raincoat over my old cardigan. I shiver on the doorstep. With the fire crackling away, the cottage is positively cosy compared to the freezing downpour outside. I trudge out, along the path and into the dripping undergrowth.

The ford looks different. In my dream, the water ran clear and fresh and bright, the banks a motley carpet of leaves. Now, everything is dank and sodden and slimy. I squelch down, peering around for anything that looks like a stone. Eventually I see the top of something, sticking out of dying nettles and grass. In my dream, the way marker stood proud and straight, but now, it leans crookedly against the bank, half-buried.

Hesitantly, I crouch in the mud before it and push my hands through the vegetation, trying not to think about snails and slugs. My fingers brush the stone's surface; although it's deeply pitted and weathered there are no signs of any carving. *Of course there aren't,* a stern voice at the back of my mind says, *this is what happens when you let yourself get carried away, you end up cold and wet and muddy for nothing.*

Then, just as I am about to pull back, my fingers brush against an indentation in the stone. Millimetre by millimetre I follow it, as it becomes a line, a curve, another curve, what is undeniably the shape of a heart ... I push myself away, pulse racing, dead leaves clinging to my hands. Through the rain I could swear that – for an instant – I heard the faint ring of metal on stone. The hairs have sprung up on my arms, on the back of my neck. I scramble back up the muddy bank as fast as I can, not daring to look behind me. I run towards the cottage, reach for the latch, only to find that the door is already open. On the other side, a shadowy figure turns to look at me, someone with eyes as bright as hazel.

★   ★   ★

I drop the kettle onto the hob, slopping water everywhere. Jack Roscarrow stands by the fireplace, watching as I mop at it with my sleeve. He's soaked through as well, dark hair wet and tangled, a puddle collecting around his feet on the flagstones.

'Sorry for barging in uninvited,' he says. 'I thought you might not have heard me knocking, what with the rain.' He pauses, stares into the fire. 'Didn't mean to frighten you.'

'It's OK.' I shove my trembling hands into my pockets. 'What are you doing here?' There doesn't seem much point in being overly polite.

With a certain grim resignation, he raises his eyes to mine.

'I came to say sorry about my grandfather, about that whole wager thing.' He's softly spoken, an accent rounding the edges of his words. 'He's not been himself for a while now. But that's no excuse for bad manners.'

'Bad manners?' I repeat incredulously. 'Making bets about a complete stranger—'

'He doesn't mean anything by it.'

'He's been trying to drive me off!' I take a step towards him. 'How do you think that feels?'

Roscarrow runs a hand through his wet hair. 'You've got to understand,' he says, 'this place means a lot to him. He's afraid of what might happen to it. It's been in our family for generations.'

'And how was I supposed to know that?' I turn back to the stove. 'Even if I did, it was Thomasina Roscarrow's decision to rent it out, not mine. I don't deserve to be punished for it.'

Behind me, I hear him sigh. 'I know,' he says. 'I'll try and talk to him.' After a while, there's a sound of rustling. I look up to find him holding a paper bag. 'I – er – brought you some buns, by way of truce. They're saffron. Thought you might not have tried them before.' He frowns down at them. 'Though they might have got a bit damp to be honest . . .'

Since I've already made tea, it's only polite to ask him to stay. We sit on the edge of the hearth, using a couple of old forks to toast the buns over the flames.

'Haven't been down here for years,' Jack Roscarrow says, smothering a bun in butter. His eyes linger over the room, the huge table, the windowpanes stuffed with rags. 'Hasn't changed much.'

He hands over the bun and I take a bite. It's exotic and homely all at once.

'She was your grandfather's aunt?' I ask, around a mouthful. 'Thomasina?'

'Something like that. Grandpa was her closest relative, anyhow, so he checked in on her from time to time. Though she never really liked visitors. She was a strange old bird. When she looked at you sometimes, it was like she was seeing right into your bones.' He smiles. 'I used to like playing here though, as a kid, sailing paper boats through the ford.'

'So why didn't she leave Enysyule to your grandfather?' I ask, as the smell of sweet toasting bread fills the room. 'You said it had been in your family for generations.'

'Well it has, on and off,' Jack says. 'There's another old family from around here, the Tremennors.' He says the name quickly, as though it might leave a bad taste in his mouth. 'They've owned this place too on occasion. It's changed hands between us over the centuries, and no one remembers who owned it first. As to why Thomasina didn't leave it to grandfather . . .' He shakes his head. 'I'm not sure.'

He takes the toasted bun off the fork, juggling it in his hands. The space between us is filled with the scent of spices and currants.

'If it makes any difference, I'm glad it's you renting this place.' He glances up at me, face glowing from the fire. 'I mean, rather than the Tremennors.'

'Well your grandfather doesn't seem too pleased about it,' I say wryly, trying to ignore the warmth in my cheeks.

Jack stifles a laugh, his mouth full. 'Trust me, he'll choose you over a Tremennor any day. Especially once he gets to know you.' He brushes crumbs from his jumper. 'He's a stubborn old weasel but I'll talk him round.'

This time when I smile, it feels genuine.

'Thanks, Jack.'

For a few minutes, we sit in comfortable silence, listening to the rain falling outside, like sand from an hourglass. I feel Jack's eyes settle upon me, and turn to meet them, when a noise makes both of us jump; a yowl, claws on wood.

'Oh for—' I scramble to my feet and pull open the door. The cat is sitting on the step completely drenched, fur spiky with water. 'What?!' I ask when it brushes past me, meowing reproachfully. 'I didn't even see you go out!'

I turn to find Jack staring at the cat, his eyes wide. 'What's wrong?' I ask.

'Nothing, it's just . . . I haven't seen him for a long time. I thought he'd look different, that's all.'

'How old do you think he is?' The firelight is an orange glow on the cat's wet fur.

'I have no idea.' He squints at the cat, as if trying to see back through time. 'If he *is* the same cat from when I was a kid, he must be nearing twenty.'

'He can't be. Cats don't live that long.' I grab a tea towel. I don't know if the cat will like being dried, but he's dripping all over the floor. He doesn't object when I start rubbing the water from his fur. 'Maybe he's a descendent or something.'

A loud, rumbling purr starts to fill the room, competing with the sound of rain from outside. The cat shakes itself free of the tea towel and wanders over to investigate the butter dish.

'Is that what you are, Perrin?' I ask the cat, reaching out to stroke it.

Sparks crackle as my fingers meet its fur. They surge up my arm, into my mind, and then everything is darkness and I hear a thousand hearts beating, I hear creatures of scale and skin, the existence of every living thing in the valley, even the trees as they groan towards the light … I snatch my hand away, disconcerted.

'Electric shock?' asks Jack.

The cat looks up at me, yellow eyes acknowledging everything I have seen.

'Yes,' I manage to reply. Tentatively, I reach out a hand towards the cat again. After a few seconds it headbutts my palm, and this time I can only feel the gentle buzz of its purr. Just a cat, nothing more.

Before he goes, Jack helps me clear away debris from the fireplace in the bedroom, so that I don't have to spend another night in the armchair by the fire.

'If I'd known you were sleeping in a chair, I would've come down sooner.' He steps back, soot and dust clinging to his skin. 'That should do it.'

I catch his glance around the room. It looks bare, my sleeping bag thrown across the bed, a suitcase standing open on the floor.

'The rest of my stuff is coming from London,' I say hurriedly. 'Though there isn't much of it. Books, mostly. I'll make do until then.'

I can tell he wants to ask more, but he just nods and smiles.

'Let me know if you need a hand with anything,' he says by the door. 'I'm downstream most days, so I can always lend you some tools.'

'Downstream?'

'At the boatyard. I work there with Granddad. Follow the stream to the river and you'll find us.' He jams a woollen hat back over his tangled hair, smiles wryly. 'Roscarrows at the river end, for as long as anyone can remember.'

'Thank you for coming,' I tell him over the sound of the rain. 'And . . . I'm sorry I snapped at you, the other day.'

'No problem.' He grins and I find myself wishing that he would stay, the cottage cosier for his presence. He trudges away, up the lane that leads out of the valley.

'See you, Jess!' he calls over his shoulder.

'See you, Jack,' I murmur, into the falling rain.

Hi Mum,

Sorry for not writing sooner. I've been so busy with settling in, I completely lost track of what day it was . . . Also, there's been a bit of a problem with the electricity, so I haven't been able to charge my phone. I've been relying on candles and the gas hob. I know you'd hate that, but actually, I'm starting to quite enjoy the disconnected life. I've been writing longhand, the way I used to, and it turns out – without the distractions of the city and the Internet – I can write pretty fast. Every day, I sit at the kitchen table and feel myself falling into a world that's somewhere between reality and imagination, waking and dreaming.

I know what you're going to ask. No, I haven't spoken to him at all. I don't have any signal, and anyway, why would I want to? We said everything we needed to say before I left London.

Here's something else to horrify you: no supermarket for fifteen miles! I get my bread from the bakery, eggs and honey from an honesty stall up the lane, and anything else from the village shop, which sells just about everything. And sure, sometimes I miss the falafel shop down the road, or lunch in Soho, but that's just part of this whole change, isn't it?

Hot water isn't working yet either. I won't pretend to have made my peace with that one. Hopefully they'll get it sorted

*soon. My hair hasn't felt clean for days. I found a tin bath in
the laundry room. My new friend Jack told me that people
used to wash in it, in front of the fire ... I might have to brave
it at some point.*

*He and his grandfather are my nearest neighbours, about a
mile away through the woods. Jack's nice, though I might
have my work cut out for me with the old man. The rest of the
village is full of interesting characters: historians, nurses,
teachers, shipwrights, smugglers ... Maybe even friends.*

*You remember the weird conditions of the tenancy? Well,
I've now met my new housemate: he's aloof and mysterious
and very handsome. He hogs my sleeping bag, wakes me up
in the middle of the night, and sometimes leaves me presents
of half-eaten mice. His name is Perrin.*

The cursor flashes, waiting for me to continue. I stare at it,
possible confessions running through my head. *And ... I've
been having these dreams. They show me things I couldn't possibly have known, the faces of people long dead. Sometimes they
turn me into smoke until I fill the valley, sometimes they give me
claws and teeth until I know what it is to hunt. Sometimes I find
myself sitting awake at night, listening for songs that can't exist ...*

With a sigh, I hold down the backspace key. I can't write
that, to my family or anyone else. At best they'll think I'm
delusional, that being alone at Enysyule has warped my
already overactive imagination. At worst, they'll be on the
next train down here, ready to hustle me back to the city with
fears about my mental state.

Instead, I just attach a photo I took of the cottage on the
day I arrived, leaves blazing behind it, windows glinting in
the sun. *Wish you were here,* I write, wondering whether that's
true.

I hit send and look around Lanford's only café, although
'café' is a loose term for a place that sells fishing tackle and

firewood, printer cartridges and wetsuits and homemade bean wine, as well as being the Post Office. But there's always coffee and slabs of cake on the go, and even more temptingly: wifi. I haven't checked my emails for days. Even looking at the number by the inbox makes me feel queasy. I stab at the last piece of carrot cake and scroll through them, before I change my mind.

One from my agent, asking how I've settled in. Another from my editor, checking that I'm still on track for the holiday deadline. I send back a brief and cheerful message assuring him that I am, wondering if he'll be able to tell that I'm lying. Below that is another message, one that makes my heart turn heavy in my chest. A familiar name, the subject line, *last things*.

I hover my cursor over it, feeling as though the new world I've built for myself over the past few weeks is about to crumble.

'Jess!' someone calls, and I snap my eyes away from the message.

'Woah,' says Alexander, taking a step back, 'ice stare! Sorry, if I'm disturbing you, I'll—'

'No.' I try to correct the look on my face into a smile. 'It's OK, I just . . . got an email I didn't particularly want.'

'Not bad news?' he asks, frowning. He looks smart today, in dark jeans and a shirt and a waxed jacket.

'No, nothing like that.' I hesitate. 'Ex-boyfriend stuff.'

He raises his eyebrows in understanding. 'Are you OK? Need another piece of cake?'

I push the empty plate aside and try to laugh. It sounds weak, but at least I don't feel like crying any more. 'No thanks.'

'Was it recent?' he asks, pulling out the chair opposite.

'Not really. A few months ago.' I sigh and close the laptop. 'It's all right, we both just changed. Especially me, apparently, since I started writing full-time. He said he wanted the old me back, he didn't understand that—' I cut myself off. 'Sorry. You don't want to hear about this.'

'I asked, didn't I? Listen though, I think I can cheer you up.' He's repressing a grin, like a child with a new joke. I feel myself smiling in response.

'You seem very sure.'

'Well,' he leans in, and I catch a breath of aftershave, rich and musky. 'I heard you were having a problem with your electricity.'

'Yes. Michaela said she would talk to Mr Roscarrow about the substation on his land. And then Jack Roscarrow came to see me. He's going to talk to his grandpa too. So between them, I think it's all sorted.'

Alexander frowns slightly. 'Oh. Look, I don't want to imply that they'd *forgotten* about it, Jess but . . . when I heard what was going on, I asked a friend of a friend who works for the grid to look into it. Turns out it's a really simple fix. They showed up to do it yesterday, but old Roscarrow was there, causing trouble.'

Disappointment flutters through me. I thought, after Jack's visit, that I was making progress with the old man. 'What do you mean, causing trouble?'

Alexander grimaces. 'He'd blocked the entrance to his land, where the substation is, so the electricity guys couldn't get in. Said that he wouldn't let them pass without written authorisation. Luckily, when they showed up again today, I happened to be passing, so I took him aside, and . . . had a quiet word.'

'A quiet word?'

He shrugs. 'Yeah. He might be a drunk, but he's not a lunatic. I just told him that he was being unreasonable, that you're a wonderful person and that he needs to give you a chance.'

My cheeks flare. 'And that's all it took?' I ask. 'He let them fix it? It's working?'

Alexander leans back, grinning. 'Should be.'

'Thank you so much!'

He waves a hand, looking pleased. 'Anyone would've done it.'

I think of Michaela's idle threats to 'have a word' with Roscarrow, Jack's promise to talk to his grandfather that also seems to have been empty. 'Anyone didn't,' I point out. 'You did.'

'Well . . .' he ruffles his hair self-consciously. 'Hey, it's the party tomorrow. Will you come?'

'I'm not sure,' I murmur, though it's beginning to sound increasingly tempting. 'None of my stuff has arrived from London yet. I'll have nothing to wear.'

'Not a problem, it's a costume party. Just wear black and say you're a cat.'

My hand hovers over the breaker switch. Days ago, the prospect of no electricity was horrifying. Now, part of me has got used to the candles, the hob, the sheets of paper for writing. What if electricity changes the cottage, changes the feeling of escape I've found here?

Don't be ridiculous, I tell myself, and push the switch. In the instant it takes for electricity to rush through the circuits, I think I hear something, a voice singing, a snatch of music from a different decade, a flash of green near the fireplace. I turn: only the wall lights flickering in their tarnished sconces.

But music – I can still hear music, a low warbling that fuzzes with static. Slowly, I make my way up the stairs. The sound is coming from the second bedroom, the room full of junk that I've been into only once. I push open the door, flick on the light. It was too dark to see much in here last time. Now, I notice an armchair and a table, beneath the window.

A radio stands there, next to a stack of books and a folded newspaper.

I reach down and touch the radio's dials. It's an old-fashioned thing, the face embellished with faraway names, *Warsaw, Paris, Moscow* . . . The song has vanished now, melted into the white noise of the in-between. How many hours did the old woman spend sitting in this chair, staring out at the valley? Was she reading this newspaper on the day she died? I pick it up. It's from around six months ago, though the print has already started to fade in the sun. It's folded over on an article headed *TREMENNOR SUBMITS MARINA PLANS*. A photograph is printed beneath it, a suited man on the steps of a grand house. A laugh escapes me. Someone – the old woman, I'm guessing – has carefully inked devil horns and fangs onto his face, a forked tail from the rear of his suit. Not for the first time, I wish I could have met her.

That name, though, Tremennor. I've heard it somewhere before. What did Jack say? Something about the other family, who once owned the cottage . . . *It's changed hands between us over the centuries, and no one remembers who owned it first.* Downstairs, the hand-drawn map is where I left it, tucked into the dresser. I unfold it gently. This time, at the edge of the map I notice a wavy line, like water. Along it, is the word *Roscarrow*, written in tiny letters. I smile. *Roscarrows at the river end, as long as anyone can remember.*

In the middle of the page is the Perranstone. At the point where the holly grove meets the wood, someone has drawn an ornate letter 'T' at the end of a dotted line. I follow it down the Western edge until I find another word. *Tremennor.*

Roscarrow and Tremennor, and Enysyule between them. I stare at the map, feeling like I'm missing something, some secret, woven from time and blood and memory, passed down, over hundreds of years.

★   ★   ★

Land remembers. Not in the way that humans do, their memories floating upon the world. Land drinks, land distils, leaving only the brightest parts, a few tangled threads of a vast and intricate design that cannot be clearly seen, only felt by those who know how to look.

*   *   *

The radio is broken. It doesn't settle on one station, but drifts between frequencies, picking up wisps of song, voices laughing, breezy advertisements. Most of all the slow, endless hiss of static; waves filled by waves filled by waves.

Lulled by the sound, my eyes drift closed. Slowly, so slowly that I don't even notice at first, the hiss grows deeper, until it merges with a creaking noise, like the deck of a ship or storm-lashed branches. But when I last looked outside the night was still and calm . . .

I open my eyes, only for an icy wind to blast them full of tears, force them closed. All at once my heart is pounding with fright and urgency. I reach out and my fingers sink into mud, cold and clogged with rotting leaves. Blind in the darkness, I stagger to my feet. Fabric drags at my legs as I break into a run, plunging through the undergrowth, searching for the path through the valley. Winter trees snag at my hair and rip it from its pins. *Take them,* I think, through the thundering of blood in my head, *take them, only please, let me reach the other side.*

A shout echoes through the trees, and I look back. Distantly I can see the glow from the cottage, torchlight flaring all around it. The glance costs me; a tree root sends me sprawling headlong onto the path, my hands scraping on cobbles, my feet tangling in petticoats. And then I see it, a black shape up ahead, shadow on shadow, eyes like the phosphorescence of the sea.

Perrin. If I had any breath I'd sob with relief. Instead, I clamber to my feet and follow him into the darkness. He pauses when I stumble, races ahead when the path is clear until the worn cobbles slope downhill, and I know we must be close. Even so, it takes me by surprise, as it always does. The Perranstone.

I squeeze through the gap in the holly and fall to my knees before it. The cat appears at my side, yowling urgently. I scoop him into my arms and bury my face in his night-cold fur.

Someone calls my name from beyond the holly trees. A sliver of light appears there, illuminating a man's face, white and drawn with fear, a dark lanthorn in his hand. He beckons and I stagger to my feet, holding Perrin tight.

That's when the thunder comes, and I don't know if it's the sound of my own scream or the noise of the wind or the whistle of the flintlock ball as it grazes the side of the stone and sends chips flying. I search the darkness beyond, terrified that the man with the lanthorn has been hit, but he only stands frozen, staring over my shoulder.

I turn to see the flames of torches fast approaching, violent in the night. Through the wind I hear dogs baying for blood. Perrin tenses in my arms. It is useless to run; they will hunt us down. The man beyond the holly calls my name again. I shake my head, and wait upon my pursuers. They will not step into the clearing. They are too afraid. The horses balk and will not be urged on. The dogs, too, have sense; they snarl and whimper and will not cross.

A voice shouts my name, my full name this time. It echoes obscenely through the night. They fling words at me, about the devil and my crimes and God's command. None of that changes what is true: it is not me they want. It is my land. Behind me, the man with the lanthorn calls a final time. I shake my head again, whisper for him to run, hoping the wind will carry my voice to him. It must, because the light flickers, metal slides over glass and his face is gone, swallowed by the darkness. I set Perrin down, tell him to run too. His eyes flare, then he melts away, as though he never was. A shred of relief, like a rivulet of water to a parched tongue.

I have no choice but to face my fate. I walk towards the men, and with every step the smell of them grows stronger, pitch and sweat and stale alcohol in dry mouths. In the torch-light I see the squire on his fine horse, I see the priest staring down, I see the men of Lanford, who on this night many years ago patted my head and called me *cheel vean* and gave me Allantide apples. Now, ready to hunt me like a fox.

Their hands make the sign of the cross as I stop at the edge of the clearing, between the holly trees. I look up at the squire, their leader. He stares down, his face cold as the stone saints in the church. He signals with the pistol.

Needles of pain dig into my flesh as Perrin bounds up onto my shoulder and leaps for the man, spitting with rage. The horse bucks and screams and I catch one glimpse of the man's face in the torchlight, his eye raked with blood. There are cries, the words *demon* and *devil*. I don't wait to see more. Instead, I turn and plunge into the holly trees, even though I know their branches will tear my skin, that the dogs will be on my heels long before I make the river . . .

Cold air slaps my face. I gulp at it, confused. Ahead of me there is nothing but darkness and silence. No coarse yells, no torches or horses or holly trees. I was running, wasn't I? My heart is thundering, breath coming fast, misting in front of my face.

Out of nowhere, two eyes appear, like quicksilver in the blackness. *Perrin*, I want to cry with relief. He trots towards me and it's only then that I realise I'm standing in the open doorway of the cottage, with the fire burning to embers and upstairs the noise of the radio, still hissing. I look down to find Perrin regarding me, his yellow eyes grave. I look down further. My feet are filthy, covered with mud and clinging leaves from the wood ... Fear swamps me as I slam the door and bolt it, run for the stairs, for the bed and my sleeping bag, where I curl, trying to stop the shaking in my limbs.

A weight lands on the bed next to me, and I tense, but then I hear a low *mew*, feel a paw patting at my head through the fabric. I'm still too scared to uncurl myself, and eventually I feel Perrin settle down, warm against my back. He begins to purr and that sound banishes the night terrors, eases me back to myself, until my mind stops racing, my breathing slows, and I sleep.

In the morning, Perrin is gone. That's the first thing I notice. I open my eyes. Grey light streams in beneath the curtains. My head feels like it's stuffed with cotton wool. Groggily, I haul myself up onto an elbow. There are a few black hairs on the outside of my sleeping bag, but apart from that—

The memory of last night hits me like a breaking wave. Fear, and flight and torches ... I scrabble my legs out of the sleeping bag, look down at my feet. They're clean. Not a trace of winter mud upon them. I slump back, a hand over my eyes. This place. My imagination.

I check my phone, charged at last. It's late, later in the day than I would usually get up. As I pass the junk room, I notice that the radio is still on, stuck on its endless whisper. I turn it off.

Perrin doesn't appear for his usual breakfast of tuna. I try not to think about it, try to busy myself with cleaning and sorting, though part of me is desperate for him to jump down from the scullery window, which I leave open for him now, desperate to look into his eyes and see what he saw, last night. *He didn't see anything,* I tell myself severely, *except you, standing in the door like a madwoman.*

It isn't until my phone bleeps with a message, picking up a stray scrap of signal, that I realise the date: October 31st. Halloween. No wonder my imagination has been going haywire. I don't have time to ponder it, because – my phone belatedly informs me – I have four missed calls and two irate messages from the courier company. They tell me that they've left my boxes at the top of the lane and that they can't be held accountable for any damage or loss if I don't answer my phone. Outside, the first flecks of rain hit the windows.

My memories of the dream fade as I ferry box after box along the lane, down the rough path at the edge of the valley and into the cottage. Even with the assistance of an old wheelbarrow from the woodshed, it takes most of the afternoon. By the time I lift the final box, the light is beginning to fade. Alex's party will be starting soon. I shouldn't go, I have to do some writing, or I'll get behind. Besides, life is already complicated enough.

I shove the wheelbarrow down the path. All Hallows Eve. What did Dan call it, that time in the pub? *Allantide. Nos Kalan Gwav, the first night of winter, where spirits walk the earth and we light our fires, to keep away the darkness that's to come . . .*

A shiver crosses my skin, and I stop dead on the path. If I went down to the Perranstone, what would I see? A face watching from the woods, the mark of a pistol shot, the footprints of a woman, hunted on this night, hundreds of years ago—?

I nearly jump out of my skin when the phone buzzes in my pocket.

Evening, ma'am! Pick you up at 7? A.

*   *   *

Allantide. Nos Kalan Gwav. Whatever name it goes by – and it has many – it is a night of fire and thunder, a death-roar of the old year. Eyes flash, teeth are bared, paws leap and twist. Come dance, the night calls, come run and roll and tear at the world until the cockcrow sends us home . . .

★　　　★　　　★

Perrin sits on the windowsill as I get ready for the party. Every so often, his tail swishes, his ears prick up, as though he is listening to voices I cannot hear, conversations that were concluded decades ago.

I *don't* go dressed as a cat. Instead, from a box of clothes, packed at the end of my past life, I pull a long, black dress. It's creased and crumpled, but hopefully that won't show. I gather up my chin-length hair, pin the curls at the back of my head. It isn't until I shake out a dark red shawl and cross it over my chest that I realise: I'm dressed in the same colours as the woman from my dream.

'Who was she, Perrin?' I ask distantly, as I stand at the tiny bedroom mirror, lining my eyes, for the first time in weeks.

Behind me, Perrin lets out a low noise, almost a growl. He's staring intently at something through the glass.

'Perrin?' I put down the eye pencil and go to look. I can see squares of light from the windows, cast onto the garden path. I rest a hand on his back.

For a second I'm caught in a rush of sound; a thundering like drums, like blood beating in my ears, then Perrin is gone, leaping from the sill and dashing down the stairs for the scullery window.

'Perrin!' I call. It's no use, I hear the squeak and thud of the frame. A moment later, tyres crunch on the path, and a pair of headlights streak crazily across the valley.

Alexander beams when I open the door, showing off a pair of plastic fangs.

'Hi,' he says with difficulty. 'Oo 'ook 'mazin'!'

'Thanks,' I laugh. 'As do you. I think.' Alex has gone all out. He's wearing a smoking jacket, a deerstalker hat with wolf ears protruding from its brim. A pair of fake sideburns and wolf make-up completes the look. 'What are you?'

He makes an exasperated noise and takes out the teeth. 'And I thought you were a literary sort. I'm the Hound of the Baskervilles, of course.' He drops the teeth into his pocket and looks around. 'You know, I don't think I've ever been down here at night. Despite the dares.'

'Didn't you Lanford kids have anything better to do than dare each other about this place?' I laugh, locking the door.

'It's just . . . never mind. Ready to go?'

He's driven here in a Land Rover, the only vehicle able to tackle the valley's rough track.

'You're not *still* scared are you?' I tease as I climb inside, forgetting my own fear, only last night.

'No,' he grimaces. 'Well, maybe a bit. Sorry, this place has always given me the creeps. I'm sure it'll be different,' he says hurriedly, starting the engine, 'when you've had a chance to make it your own.'

I look back over my shoulder, as the valley drops into darkness behind us, wondering whether I'll ever be able to feel like it is truly mine. But my brooding is soon lost in the jolting of the car. We're thrown from side to side on our way up the hill, until I'm laughing at the ridiculousness of it all. Alexander – or Alex as I can't help calling him – is good company, and by the time we turn out of the lane, I feel some of my preoccupation dropping away.

'So, where is this party of yours?' I ask, over the roar of the engine.

'Not far,' he grins, 'just on the other side of the village.'

I can't tell if he's being nonchalant, or deliberately cryptic. Soon, though, we're talking about my writing, about how I plan to spruce up the cottage. We're driving through Lanford now, and the town looks wonderful. Windows and doors are draped with fake cobwebs, candles flicker on doorsteps inside carved pale vegetables that definitely aren't pumpkins.

'What are they?' I ask, spotting a particularly gruesome example.

'Turnips,' says Alex, as we pull up alongside the pub, to let another car pass. 'We're Cornish. No pumpkins for us.'

As I laugh, I see Jack emerge from the pub with a few other people. He's holding a pint that has been dyed bright orange. I knock on the window and wave. His eyes meet mine for a second. Then his face drops into a scowl and he turns away, standing with his back to the car until we drive off. Hurt twists through me, and confusion.

'What was that about?' I murmur, peering into the wing mirror.

'What was what?'

'Jack Roscarrow. I don't understand, he was so friendly the other day.'

Alex is quiet for a minute, navigating a road that runs up behind the village.

'Sorry, Jess,' he says eventually, 'that's probably my fault.'

'What do you mean?' I look across at him in the darkness of the car.

'Jack and I have never … got on very well,' he says awkwardly. 'Ever since we were kids. He's the moody sort, you know? Got a chip on his shoulder about certain things.' He takes a sharp left, into a dark lane. '*And* he's probably pissed off that I sorted out your electricity before he could be bothered to do anything about it.'

I nod, trying to reconcile my memory of bright hazel eyes and a cold rainy afternoon with what's just happened. Then, through the headlights, I see a pair of gateposts approaching. Grand ones. A huge bunch of red and orange balloons is tied to each, and beneath them, a carved plaque:

TREMENNOR ESTATE
PRIVATE PROPERTY

'Tremennor,' I whisper. The name brings with it an inexplicable feeling of unease. 'Why are we here? I thought you said the party was at your place?'

'It is,' Alexander looks sheepish, 'well, not *literally* my place, not yet. I live in the coach house.'

I can see the manor now, emerging from beyond dark hedges. Before, I only glimpsed its tower. Now, I see it's a tall, angular place, built from grey stone, lit by softly glowing windows. Downhill, the gardens merge with the wood. Somewhere, on the other side of those trees is Enysyule.

'You're a *Tremennor*?' I can't hide the shock in my voice. 'Why didn't you tell me?'

'Because I didn't want to scare you off!' Alex swings into a U-shaped courtyard at the side of the house, already littered with cars. 'Honestly, Jess, if you thought the rumours about you were bad, you should hear what they have to say about *us*.' He jerks his head back towards the village. 'Five hundred years worth of grudges doesn't make for easy friendships.' He sighs, turns off the engine. 'I just wanted to be me for once. Without all the baggage.'

He turns away, and for a moment, I think he's upset. Then he looks back, wolf teeth in place.

'I'll 'ake it up 'o 'ou,' he drools, so entreatingly that before I know it I'm laughing, forgetting all about lands and boundaries and dreams.

'All right,' I say, climbing out. 'But leave me alone in there and I'll kill you.'

Tremennor House feels a thousand miles from Enysyule, yet oddly familiar. Just like the cottage, I can see history in its every line, in the steps worn by generations of feet, in the mullioned windows and carved gables. Alex leads the way. Candles flicker on either side of the path, guiding us towards a heavy arched door. Above, a square tower looms from the roof.

'No wonder you have Halloween parties here,' I murmur, as Alex pushes his way inside. 'It's like something from an Ann Radcliffe novel.'

'Not Halloween, *Allantide*,' he says. 'Come on, they're getting started without us.'

I try not to gawp as we enter the hallway. The place looks like a museum. There are animal heads and weaponry, even a shield on one wall. I stop to look at its design: an ochre rectangle with a circle through the middle, a stripe of red behind it. My skin prickles with recognition.

'Is that . . .?' I stand on tiptoe to look closer.

'The stone? Yeah, we're tied to that old thing.' He glances up. 'It's in the name, Tre-mennor – men of the stone.' His nudge nearly sends me flying. 'Ironic it's on your land, eh?'

'Alex!' someone shouts, and he ushers me into a wide, high-ceilinged room, lit by candles and lanterns. Shiny red apples line the mantelpieces; bats on strings bounce from gilded wall sconces. I can't see any speakers, though they must be hidden away somewhere because 'Thriller' is bouncing incongruously from the wood-panelled walls.

One end of the room has been turned into a bar. On our way there, Alex introduces me to people whose names I instantly forget. Everyone is in fancy dress. It's disconcerting and intoxicating all at once. Eyes follow me as I cross the room, whispers trailing behind us. I feel very aware of my crumpled dress, musty from being packed, of my scuffed boots, my messy hair.

'Why are they all looking?' I mumble to Alex as we reach a huge table stocked with drink; bottles of champagne on ice, kegs of beer and cider, a wide bowl filled with something red.

'They're just curious,' he says, picking up a couple of glasses. 'Beautiful, mysterious strangers don't often show up in Lanford.'

Embarrassed, I pull the shawl a bit tighter about my chest.

Alex must notice my discomfort. 'Here,' he says, handing me a glass. 'This should help.'

'What is it?' I peer down into the pale red liquid.

'Punch,' he clinks his glass with mine. 'Welcome to the neighbourhood.'

The drink is sweet and tastes powerfully of apples. I feel its effect almost immediately, tingling through me, washing away some of my reticence at being in this place. I drink the rest of the glass in one.

Alex raises his eyebrows. 'Girl after my own heart,' he says, and does the same.

With glasses refreshed, he takes me on a tour of the house. We pass through parlours and billiard rooms, hallways and a library, where wooden shelves capture the light and send it back in a warm, heady glow.

Alex talks me through everything, stopping to greet people and introduce me. I find myself staring at him, in his bizarre wolf costume, and feel a pang of sympathy. I can't imagine growing up, being a child in a place like this, with a name half a millennium old hanging over your head. No wonder he sees it as baggage.

Eventually we end up outside, sitting in a sunken garden around a fire pit with a group of younger people I assume are Alex's friends. As he predicted, they're all immediately curious about who I am and why I'm there. I get the usual range of odd looks when I say I'm renting Enysyule, but soon, with the punch flowing, everyone starts to relax.

Even with the fire, it's a cold night, and Alex finds a blanket, slings it over both our shoulders. *People will think we're together*, my mind warns. I ignore it. The feeling of his arm, pressed against mine, sends sparks of possibility through my body.

'So what about London?' a guy called TJ booms from across the fire. He's dressed in a top hat, his suit ripped down one side. 'Has it always been home, Jess?'

I shrug. 'Not really. We used to live in Manchester. We only moved to London after Dad died.' I take another sip of punch, wave away their apologies. 'It was a long time ago,' I tell them. 'After he was gone, Mum wanted to live in a capital city again. She grew up in Istanbul, said she missed the noise, the crowds, but I think she just wanted a fresh start.' The thought of my mum's quick, rounded accent brings a pang of homesickness. 'She's always said that London is like ivy, it grows and it grows and no one remembers where it all came from or where the roots are.'

Alex is quiet, staring into the fire. He told me earlier that his own parents are divorced; his mum has lived in New York for years. I wonder if all this talk makes him miss her, too. I nudge him with my elbow and receive a smile in return.

'Did your mum mind you moving here?' asks a girl in a spandex cat-woman outfit. I think her name is Maisy.

'Yes, she minded. She's horrified,' I laugh, fishing a piece of apple out of my drink. 'So is my sister. They're city people, through and through. I think they're hoping I'll give up on the idea and come home.'

'Well I won't allow it,' TJ says, slapping his leg. 'You're the most interesting thing to happen around here for yonks. Even if Alexander here *did* somehow manage to meet you first—'

'I, err, where's the bathroom?' I ask quickly, deflecting the inevitable questions.

Inside, the house is darker than before, the party louder, more raucous. *Turn left,* Alex said, *straight on, third door on the right*. I push open what is hopefully the bathroom door, and walk in on a zombie, mid-wee.

'Sorry!' I bolt outside, cringing in the darkness of the hall.

Alex said there was another bathroom, at the top of the stairs. I return to the hall, with its Tremennor shield, its walls adorned with memorabilia. The sight of a flintlock pistol sends a shiver through me. Tentatively I begin to climb the huge, old wooden staircase.

It's darker up here, just one or two small table lamps lighting the way. For some reason I feel like I'm trespassing, but my bladder insists that finding a bathroom is an urgent matter. Thankfully it's exactly where Alex said it was. On my way out, I close the door as quietly as possible, ready to hurry back down the stairs, hopefully without being noticed.

As I turn away, something catches my eye. One of the doors further along the corridor is now open; light is spilling onto a painting that hangs on the opposite wall. Despite my better judgement, I find myself walking towards it, my head fuzzy with alcohol. It shows a figure in an ornate coat, a white collar high to his neck. One hand rests on a musket, the other on a dog's head. *Godfield Tremennor*, a tarnished plaque reads. I look up into the portrait's face.

The man from my dream looks down, his expression cold, and for an instant I'm back at the Perranstone, terrified, the smell of men and danger and dogs all around me . . .

A voice breaks the silence, and the dark wood disappears, replaced by the hallway, the sound of the party filtering up the stairs. Another voice joins the first, a woman's this time, slightly raised, as though in dispute. They're coming from the room behind me. I shouldn't be listening, probably shouldn't even be up here. I'm about to sneak away when I hear the word *Enysyule*.

It stops me in my tracks.

'. . . livid about it,' a man snaps. He sounds well spoken.

'Look, I know it must be frustrating for you.' I lean closer in the darkness, recognising the voice. It's Michaela Welwyn. 'I can assure you it was—'

'Don't give me that crap.' The man sounds furious. 'Why didn't you tell me you had someone coming to look at the place? I thought I'd made my intentions clear!'

'You discussed your thoughts with me, yes,' Michaela says hotly. 'But we're a *business*, Roger. I couldn't very well turn down an excellent tenant based on your vague intentions.'

'You should have told me she was coming!' he fumes. 'You know I would have got down there first! Did you really think I'd be happy to let some clueless Londoner scoop it up if I'd bloody well known?'

'I'd appreciate it if you didn't swear at me,' says Michaela. 'I wasn't expecting Miss Pike to sign the lease on the spot, but she did, so there really wasn't any time to inform you.'

'It isn't even legal.' The man's voice has turned hard. My stomach drops. What does he mean? 'Tying a place to the life expectancy of a damn *cat*. It won't hold up in court and trust me, I'm going to—'

I shift closer, trying not to miss anything, when the floor-boards groan loudly under my weight, betraying my presence.

'Yes?' the man calls, and I barely have time to take a few steps back down the corridor before the door is flung open, throwing light across me.

'I – er– sorry,' I stutter, all too aware of my red face. 'I was looking for the bathroom.'

The man is staring at me, his face taut with frustration. He's in his sixties, dressed as an aristocrat, white make-up on his face, and a gory line of blood across his neck. I hear foot-steps, and before I can turn away, Michaela steps out into the hallway. She's dressed as a very gaudy, bespectacled Cleopatra. Her heavily lined eyes widen at the sight of me. If I wasn't so bewildered, I'd laugh at the scene.

'Jess!' she says. 'I mean, Miss Pike, I didn't know you were here.'

For a second, we all stare at each other, the weight of their argument hanging between us.

'Yes,' I tell her, finding my voice. 'I . . . Alexander invited me.'

'Alexander?' the man demands with a frown. 'You came here with my son?'

'I did. Is that a problem?'

His face drops into a dry smile. 'No, no of course not. Just a surprise. He neglected to mention that he'd made your acquaintance.' He holds out a hand. 'Roger Tremennor.'

I take the proffered hand, my thoughts a blur. 'Jessamine Pike. I'm renting Enysyule.'

'So I hear.' His glance at Michaela is unmistakable.

She rallies, takes my arm and guides me towards the stairs. 'Miss Pike, here's an interesting fact: did you know that Enysyule shares a boundary with Mr Tremennor's land?'

'Yes,' I tell her, resisting the urge to take the stairs two at a time, 'the woods, on the other side of the Perranstone.'

There's a sharp silence.

'Indeed,' Tremennor says. 'Our namesake. It belonged to us once, you know, that whole valley.'

'I thought it belonged to the Roscarrows?'

He squints at me. 'Been doing some research, have you?'

'Jess!' Alex comes hurrying out of the main room, werewolf sideburns askew. He sees his father and Michaela, and stops, flushing slightly. 'Oh, Dad. This is—'

'We've already introduced ourselves,' Roger interrupts. 'Or were you planning on keeping her a secret all night?'

Alex grimaces at him, before grabbing my arm. 'Hi, Michaela,' he calls over his shoulder, dragging me away into the crowded main room. 'God, I'm sorry,' he murmurs in my ear. 'Was that awful? Dad can be prickly at times.'

The overheard conversation has left me feeling shaky. *It isn't even legal* . . . Roger Tremennor clearly wanted Enysyule, and missed out on securing it somehow. Was it just bitterness talking? I want to ask Alex, but a live band has started playing, drowning out all hope of conversation. It'll have to wait.

Alex's friend TJ cheers when he sees us. He's located a bottle of tequila from somewhere, is offering round shots. I find myself taking one, to steady myself, then another to drown out the thoughts jostling in my head, the faces of people I couldn't possibly have known, the creeping certainty that Roger Tremennor is going to be bad news . . .

When the band bursts into a raucous shanty, I let the others drag me onto the dance floor. We link arms and fling ourselves about, yelling pirate curses. Soon, a fiddle player takes over the melody. It becomes livelier, and more people join in, feet stomping and hands clapping. The music works its way into my blood, until I cease to be me, become instead a set of limbs that move with the rhythm of the dance, the way bodies have for centuries. It gets faster, the song building towards its conclusion, and our circle splits apart.

Through the crowd, I see Roger Tremennor watching me with interest, so like the man in my dream . . . I catch his eye and stumble, tripping over my dress. Alex is there to catch me. He puts his hands around my waist, spins me until everything blurs, and we could be anywhere, in any time, the young lord of Tremennor and the girl from Enysyule.

Finally, dizzy and weak with laughter, we stagger from the hall, clinging to each other for balance. Outside, the night flows like iced water into my lungs. There are a few people sitting down by the fire pit, but Alex takes my hand, pulls me out of sight into a walled garden.

'Alex, what—' I laugh, then his mouth is on mine and my breath disappears into the kiss.

'I'm sorry,' he says, breaking away, 'I've wanted to do that from the moment I saw you.'

'I . . .' I murmur, without stepping away. 'I'm new here, I only just met you.' *Your father wants Enysyule, he wants to get rid of me, just like your ancestors did.*

We stand, bodies thrumming with music and alcohol and the possibility of each other. And then, I'm kissing him back, because this is a story that's happened before, because through the thundering of my heart and the sound of our hasty breathing there's another noise, that of a knife, carving the shape of a heart; carving a broken promise into stone.

No dreams, save one, the sound of a woman's voice singing.
''Ma greun war an kelynn mar rudh 'vel an goes.'
The words sound familiar and foreign at the same time, the tune a simple one. *Kelynn*, the woman repeats, *kelynn*, and in my heart I know that it is a winter song; a song for when the fire blazes brightly, for when holly glows green against the snow . . . But it is too fragile for the waking world. As I stir, it breaks like a strand of cobweb and vanishes. For a long time I don't move a muscle, hoping it will return, hoping to fall back into it. Gradually I become aware of a pounding in my head, heaviness in my limbs. I groan and roll over, burying my face in the duvet.

Duvet – not sleeping bag. I sit bolt upright, head spinning. I see a spacious room, white-painted with exposed beams and modern, arched windows. In a rush, it all comes back to me, the dancing and the tequila, the walled garden, our escape down a candlelit path, the glasses of ice-cold vodka that seemed like such a great idea at the time, and then . . .

The blood rushes to my face as I look over. No Alex. I'm not sure whether to feel glad about that or sorry. There's a glass of water by the bed. Evidently I had enough sense to put it there before going to sleep. I drink it in one and flop back on the pillows, wishing the pounding in my head would go away so I could think properly for a minute.

Feet walk slowly up the stairs. I risk a look over the top of the duvet. Alex stands there in a pair of blue pyjamas, balancing two mugs and a plate of biscuits.

'Morning,' he says, setting a cup down beside me. 'Thought you might need this.'

'Thanks.' The smell of freshly ground coffee hits me, like a cold wave on a hot day. 'I *definitely* need it.'

'Me too,' Alex groans and sits on the edge of the bed.

I wrap my hands around the mug. 'So.'

'Um.'

'I definitely didn't plan for this to happen.'

He looks down into his mug. 'Me neither . . . are you sorry for it?'

The traces of wolf make-up left on his neck make me smile. 'I probably should be, knowing how the village gossips,' I say. 'But I'm not.'

His grin is huge in return. He puts down his mug and rolls towards me. 'Forget about the gossip,' he says, 'it's all jaffle.'

'It's *what*?' I laugh.

'Jaffle.' He makes his accent broad. 'That's Cornish that is, means a lot of old tosh.'

'Do you know any more?' The gentle, singing voice comes back to me, the song from my dream that I couldn't understand, yet felt the meaning of, all the same. Was that Cornish too?

'Only bits and pieces,' Alex says. 'Why, did you think I'd be fluent in the old tongue?'

I thump him with a pillow. 'I thought you'd know at least a bit, having lived here your whole life.' Abruptly I remember Alex's father, his eyes fixed on mine. *It belonged to us once, you know,* he'd said, *that whole valley.*

'Alex,' I say, and he must hear the change in my voice, because he puts down the pillow he had grabbed to retaliate with. 'Last night I overheard your father and Michaela talking. Is it true he wanted Enysyule?'

There's no mistaking the surprise on his face. He picks up his coffee and takes a large gulp. 'You heard him say that?'

'Yeah. He sounded pretty angry that Michaela had rented it to me instead of him.'

Alex makes a noise in his throat. 'I know he'd *talked* to Michaela about it in the past, but he hadn't actually signed anything, which is why you managed to pip him to the post. He wasn't expecting that. I think he forgets that business can't always be done with a wink and a casual word.' He drains the rest of his coffee. Is he just acting nonchalant? 'Anyway, don't take it personally. Dad's on a mission to revamp the estate. He's chasing any property within ten miles of here.' When I don't respond, his face grows serious. He reaches up, strokes a strand of hair away from my cheek. 'Look, I'm *glad* he didn't get it, OK? Otherwise I wouldn't have met you.'

Finally I nod and retrieve my own coffee.

'Can I . . . take you out sometime?' he asks as I drink. 'I'd like to.'

Every rational thought is telling me that this isn't a good idea, reminding me that I don't know whether he is telling the truth about his father, and yet . . . I can't help feeling like I've stumbled into something important, something that's *meant* to happen.

'I don't see why not,' I say.

He lets out a whoop. 'How about this afternoon? The weather's meant to be good, we could go anywhere you want—' he catches himself. 'Unless, you know, you have plans?'

'There *is* somewhere I've been dying to go actually, ever since I got here. Though it's not exactly romantic.'

'That doesn't matter. Where is it?'

I feel a grin creep onto my face. 'The hardware store. The big one in Redruth.' Alex looks pained. 'What?!' I demand.

'There's so much stuff I need for the cottage and you said anywhere I wanted!'

'I did.' He kisses me on the cheek. 'All right, the hardware store it is. On the condition that we go for lunch too. Hardware shopping on a hangover is not a pleasant business, trust me.'

Perrin is waiting for me when I walk in, my arms full of screwdrivers and dusters and sugar soap. He arches his back and yawns pointedly as if to say *I see you've decided to return at last.* My face burns, still tingling with the feel of Alex's lips. When he dropped me off, he tried to persuade me to stay, to skip a day of writing and go for dinner with him instead. It was tempting, very tempting, but I had to draw the line somewhere. Plus, down the hill I could feel that Enysyule was waiting. Not to mention Perrin, who would be expecting his dinner.

'Stop giving that look,' I tell the cat. 'I can see who I like.'

Perrin makes a noise somewhere between a meow and a grunt and jumps down, heading pointedly towards the pantry with its supplies of tinned tuna. While he eats, I open a new packet of dusters and a can of furniture polish. Now that my belongings have arrived from London, there's no excuse to leave things in a mess. And anyway, I could use the distraction.

The bedroom seems the easiest place to start. There's still not much in here except the bed, the locked trunk, and my open suitcase. Polishing the headboard for the first time, I realise how beautiful it is. It's carved all over with an intricate design of leaves and berries and fits perfectly into the crooked walls. It must have been built for this place. The dark wood takes the polish I feed it and gives back a red-brown glow, like the conkers my sister and I once collected from Manchester's parks, that emerged glossy from their spiked green pockets.

Dad used to drill holes in them for us, so we could string them and play against the other kids at school.

Like the table downstairs, the bedstead bears the marks of time, generations of scuffs and scratches. I polish each one carefully. Somehow, they feel as precious as the rest of it. That done, I search through the moving boxes for sheets, pillows, bed linen, and retire my sleeping bag at last. The room instantly feels cosier. After the excitement and strangeness of the past twenty-four hours, all I want to do is crawl beneath the blankets but I force myself to walk downstairs. There's writing to be done.

As always, Perrin comes to sit beside me while I work, and I feel myself sinking gratefully into the quiet. I'm glad I haven't tried to fix the radio. The sound of the fire, the distant hoots of an owl outside and Perrin's gentle purr are company enough.

My book is growing slowly, like a seedling coaxed from the ground, inching forward every day. I find myself writing of a place that is and is not Enysyule. I take its dew-strung spiders' webs, its mercury slug trails, its layers of dust like fine fur, and weave them together with threads of illusion, strands of fantasy, like old stories from a different world. The words spill out of me, as though they are jostling to reach the ends of my fingers, and I barely have to pay attention to what I'm typing. I write and write until my eyes grow heavy, until they keep sliding closed and the words become muddied with half-dreams. I catch the laptop as it begins to fall to the floor, shove it onto the table, and stumble up the stairs to bed, to the blissfully clean sheets.

'Perrin,' I call sleepily. A black, fluffy shadow appears, and settles on my legs. 'You can't stay there,' I murmur. Perrin gives a *mrrrrp* of disagreement and begins to make dough on my knees. I'm asleep before I can even protest.

★   ★   ★

The land has its own language, where names represent what is true;
Baldhu, Halwyn, Redruth ... black mine, white moor, red ford. It is
a language that tells where dry ground becomes marsh, where
hollows wait and foxes make their homes. It knows that while paper
tears and ink fades and people forget, stone remembers.

* * *

'They tell stories, the creatures that are brave enough to come
here. They say that the old places are being lost, that roads
cut the land and leave thick scars, the earth broken open. The
tin men broke the earth too; they took it in their hands,
followed its veins of brightness and bled it, but did not drain
it. Now, the creatures tell me, there are machines bigger than
houses, stronger than a hundred horses, and they drink the
land dry. They will not come here. They cannot. This place is
guarded, it is protected by stone and spirit, it is—'

The cursor flashes at the end of the unfinished sentence.
I stare at it in disbelief, a cup of tea growing cold by my
elbow. I only intended to have a quick look over what I wrote
last night, but this . . . I have no memory of writing it, none
at all. I read it again. *Stone and spirit*, what does that even
mean? The whole paragraph sounds concerned, worried
that something might happen to the valley. Enysyule is in
my care, isn't it, at least for a year? There's nothing that can
change that. Still, I can't shake a dull, nagging sense of
unease as I highlight the text and copy it into a new document. I'll have to talk to Michaela, next time I'm in the
village.

In the meantime, regardless of what old Mr Roscarrow or
Roger Tremennor would prefer, I intend to make the cottage
my home. The days begin to fall into a pattern; tea and toast
for breakfast – tuna for Perrin – then cleaning and fixing and
sprucing in the afternoon, writing in the evening.

I begin to learn the cottage's ways. I discover bats asleep in
the outside toilet, hanging from the beams and window

ledges. I find mysterious snail trails over the flagstones in the morning, and I am, through sheer necessity, getting over my fear of spiders. Perrin doesn't mind them at all. More often than not, he'll pounce, play with them for a while before deciding to eat them, chewing methodically despite my noises of disgust.

Perrin and I seem to have reached a domestic agreement too, though he finds ways to remind me that I'm living in *his* house. Mostly this involves taking up two-thirds of the huge, carved bed, or attacking my computer mouse, as though he thinks it is his duty to try and kill it. Other times, he'll spend all night on the roof, yowling cat songs to the moon.

On these nights, my dreams are stronger than ever. They are odd, fleeting things, full of pounding hearts and wild eyes. Once, I wake with a stranger's name on my lips, which disappears the instant I try to speak it. Another time, I could swear that I surface from sleep with the taste of brandy on my tongue. The dreams always wither away in daylight, until only the feeling remains.

One day, dusting the books on the dresser and making room for my own, I find the sketchbook again, fronted by Thomasina Roscarrow's graceful signature. This time, I take a closer look. It's full of charcoal drawings, beautiful, swirling things, all shadows and shade. Some I recognise; parts of the valley, the meadow, an old broken plant pot that still sits outside the front door. The best one is a work of imagination that resonates inexplicably with my dreams. It shows a huge cat-shape, curled like smoke around the cottage. The smudges on the paper suggest long fur, gleaming eyes. I smile and stroke the corner of the page. It can only be Perrin.

He comes to keep me company later that afternoon, as I sit on the front step shaking out dusters. The season is hanging on the very edge of winter. Soon the last leaves will fall, making way for frost. Perrin surveys his valley, fur fluffed out and regal. Experimentally, I flourish the duster in front of his face. He blinks indignantly, whiskers twitching. I grin and wave it again. I can see that he's trying to resist, his paws flexing on the stone. And although he's a strange cat, he's a cat through and through; when I flourish the duster a third time he swipes at it with his paw and twists away.

My breath mists in the chill air as I laugh, hopping backwards. Perrin dances after me, all pounce and coiled spring, all flashing eye and needle claw. Finally he gets the better of me, snatches the duster from my hand. Like a flash, he picks it up in his teeth and runs away, around the side of the house. Soon, frantic ripping noises begin to fill the air.

I wipe the laughter from my eyes and am about to go indoors when I see a figure, watching through the trees. My skin leaps in alarm before I recognise the coat, the hat above it.

'Jack!' I call, forgetting his sullen behaviour outside the pub. He doesn't reply, but I hurry over anyway, hoping he's decided to be friendly again. 'Have you come for a visit? I was just about to make some tea.'

His face remains closed as ever, mouth a thin line beneath his dark stubble. He pulls an envelope from his pocket, and shoves it in my direction. 'Came to deliver this,' he says. 'That's all.'

He turns away to leave. Anxiety trickles into my stomach. 'Wait.' I take a few steps after him. 'What is it?' The envelope is plain, addressed only J. PIKE.

'It's a bill.' He doesn't look at me, just over my shoulder, at the valley.

'What for?' I start to rip open the paper.

'For damage caused to my grandfather's land,' he says. 'Those electricians drove their truck into one of the hedges. It'll have to be replanted.'

I stare at the piece of paper, at the handwritten cost in blunt, blocky letters. 'I'm ... sorry about that. I didn't ask them to—'

'No. You didn't. You got your boyfriend to take care of it.'

'*What*?'

'You know what I mean.'

'If you're talking about Alexander,' I snap, anger bubbling through the hurt, 'then no, he is not my boyfriend. But he was good enough to sort out the electricity for me. Which is more than you did, even after you promised.'

'I promised because I thought I was wrong about you,' Jack says, red high on his cheekbones. 'I *told* my grandfather and all his friends that they should be ashamed of themselves, that you were decent. Now I just look like an idiot.'

'Why?' The blood rushes to my face. 'Because I decided to spend the night with someone you have a stupid grudge against?'

Jack is silent, jaw tight. For a few, heavy seconds, we just stare at each other.

'Well,' he says at last, 'you've made it clear how you intend to get on here. Please pay that bill within two weeks.'

Then he's gone, striding away up the path, coat hunched around him.

'He was so *rude*,' I call over the noise of the shower. 'You should've heard him. And that bill – if I hadn't seen him he would've just left it for me to find, no explanation, nothing.'

I let the powerful jets of water run over my head, sluicing the shampoo from my hair. I wish the bad feeling would rinse away just as easily.

'This is my fault,' I hear Alex say from outside. 'I shouldn't have got involved.'

'No, it isn't,' I wipe water from my eyes and peer around the frosted glass, 'you were just trying to help. *They're* the

ones who have been making things difficult for me, right
from the beginning.'

He sighs. 'Still, this isn't about you, Jess. Not really. The
Roscarrows have always been trouble. If it weren't this business about the cottage, it'd be something else. Your moving
here has just . . . stirred things up again, that's all.'

My noise of disbelief echoes from the tiles.

'Well, they're trying pretty damn hard to get rid of me.' I
scrub at my hair again. 'Did you know that Michaela's been
trying to find a plumber to come down and take a look at the
boiler? Every one of them said no. I have a feeling I know
why.'

'Dad's got a plumber on retainer for the estate. I can ask
him if you want.'

I hesitate, letting the rush of water fill the silence. I don't
want to be indebted to Roger Tremennor for anything.
'Thanks. I'd rather try and sort this out on my own.'

'Suit yourself. Are you ever getting out of there?'

'No way,' I duck back under the water. 'This is heaven.
You'll have to drag me out.'

Much, much later I lie awake in the darkness. Despite the
warmth of Alex beside me, despite the wine we've drunk and
the smoothness of the sheets, I can't sleep. I'm missing the
sounds of the cottage, I realise, its creaks and clanks as it
settles for the night, the calling of the owls and Perrin's
rumbling purr. I listen and listen. All I can hear is the hum of
electricity, the hiss of the dishwasher, Alex's breathing. Before
I left London it was always like this; I would lie awake with
my brain churning in the darkness, thoughts growing ever
blacker as the night wore on. It hasn't happened for weeks,
but now, I toss and turn and fret until false dawn begins to
filter through the blinds. When I do finally fall asleep, my
dreams are thin, flimsy things; echoes of the day, words of
scorn, a pair of bright hazel eyes . . .

'Jess? You OK?'

A hand is shaking me.

'What?' I murmur groggily. Alex leans on the side of the bed. He's already dressed, in a shirt and smart trousers.

'What time is it?' I grope for my phone.

'Time to be up, I'm afraid.' He smiles. 'You all right? You look knackered?'

'Didn't sleep very well.' I shove my hair off my face. 'Sorry. I'm a wreck this morning.'

He reaches for my hand. 'Still worrying about Roscarrow? If you want I can have a word with the tradesmen in the village. A lot of them do work for my father.'

'No,' I rub at my eyes, 'I have to do this myself. I'm not going anywhere. They'll just have to get used to me sooner or later.'

'That's the spirit.' He hauls me upright. 'Come on. I've got to go and meet Dad and some investors about this new marina thing, but I can drop you in town to do battle with the locals.'

Lanford is bustling; at least, as bustling as a secluded village at the far end of Cornwall can be. A very old and rickety cherry picker is parked, blocking the main street. I stop to watch as a young man – who has drawn the short straw – is hoisted aloft, foot by excruciating foot. He's festooned with cables and wires, and starts trying to throw the end of one over the gable of the pub. The wind gusts down the street, the cherry picker sways and the young man yelps, holding on for dear life. I spot Pete, Liza's cousin from the pub, staring up and shaking his head. He's wearing a high-vis jacket, looks like he's supposed to be directing traffic, although most of the motorists have also stopped to watch.

'What's going on?' I ask, as the young man attempts to lasso the gable again.

'Christmas lights,' Pete says, without looking down. 'Same bloody palaver, every year. Left Liam! To the left!'

I leave them to their fun and take refuge from the weather in the village shop. It's poky and narrow, but the shelves seem to hold everything, from tights to pencils to locally grown onions. I wander around, filling a basket with milk and butter and biscuits. There are half a dozen tins of tuna left on the shelf. I take four, hesitate, then take the others as well.

'Afternoon, Miss Pike,' the man at the counter greets, laying aside what looks like a book on medieval weaponry. We've never been properly introduced, although around here, that doesn't make much difference. I try not to blush at the thought of what the village gossips have been saying about Alex and me.

'Afternoon, Reg,' I tell him, reading the faded nametag that's pinned to his jumper. 'How's everything with you?'

He looks at me quizzically over his glasses.

'Oh, ticking along, Miss Pike, ticking along.' He begins to pick items out of my basket, scrutinising them before ringing them through the till.

'They're hanging the Christmas lights out there,' I tell him, for something to say.

'Are they now?' He walks off with a packet of biscuits in his hand to peer through the front window. 'See they got young Liam Bligh up there. Never could tell his left from his right, that boy.' He watches for another minute or so, then returns to the packing. 'Let's hope they do a proper job. I suppose you won't be here for Christmas, Miss Pike?'

He drops the biscuits into my bag. I feel my temper flare.

'Why not? This is where I live.'

Reg inclines his head. 'Didn't mean to offend, just thought you might be spending it upcountry with your family, is all. Where was it? London?'

'Oh,' I watch as he rings through a box of teabags. 'Yes, London. Though we don't usually do much for Christmas.'

Outside, the wind blasts along the street, flattening people's hair and toppling bins. A flurry of rain hits the glass. I look up to find Reg staring into the basket, as if it pains him.

'Got a liking for tuna, have you, Miss Pike?' he says. 'I'll order more in, if so.'

I look at the half-dozen tins of the stuff. 'It's – er – not for me. It's for the cat. He won't eat normal cat food.'

Reg's face brightens. 'For old Perrin? He's taken to you then?'

A smile escapes me. 'I think he's decided I'll do for a housekeeper.'

'Good, that's good.' Reg nods seriously, ringing up the total on the till. 'Listen, don't bother with this rubbish,' he looks disdainfully at the tuna. 'Get yourself down to where the fishing boats put in in the mornings. Say I sent you. They'll give you some nice scraps. It's what Miss Roscarrow did for years.'

'I'm guessing they know Perrin as well?'

Reg chuckles. 'He's always been a fish cat. Like as not they'll give you some salmon for him at Christmas.'

I find myself laughing too, buoyed by his kindness. Reg smiles at me over his glasses. 'Say you need a plumber for the cottage?'

Of course, he knows that too. 'Yes,' I tell him cautiously, 'though we haven't had much luck. Seems they're rarer than gold dust around here.'

'You might try old Amity Hesketh, next village over.' He lowers his voice, though there's no one to hear us. 'She's not zackly what you'd call a plumber, more a handywoman, but she'd do you something, sure enough.' He jerks his head. 'Her card's in the window there.'

'Thanks,' I tell him, surprised.

He nods his head once, satisfied.

'Reg?' I ask after a moment, handing some money over. 'Who owned Enysyule before Miss Roscarrow? Do you know?'

'All depends what you mean by before.' He counts out change from the till. 'Backalong it might've been the Roscarrows,' he shrugs, 'before that it might've been Tremennors. Wudden like to say.'

The door opens with a jingle, letting in two old ladies, who stare at me like I've grown another head. 'Thanks, Reg,' I tell him, gathering up my shopping. 'See you again.'

Outside, the wind nearly knocks me off my feet. Next to the café-post-office-bait-shop I see Liza, wrestling with an inside-out umbrella.

'Liza!' I yell through the wind, and wade over, into the shelter of the doorway.

'Oh, Jess. How are you doing? We haven't seen you for a while.' Her voice sounds rather cool.

'No, well, I've been . . . busy,' I flush, 'with writing, and the cottage. There's been a lot of tidying up to do.'

'Yes, of course,' she says politely.

We stand in awkward silence, watching a plastic bag sail past, like a giant, airborne jellyfish.

'Jess—' Liza starts.

'If this is about Alexander—'

'I'm not judging,' she says hurriedly, 'it's just that . . .' She stops, looking ahead. 'Oh dear.'

I follow her gaze. From across the road, a figure is staring at us. An old man, his oilskin cape lashing around him like wings. My stomach twists in apprehension. Mel Roscarrow. I start to take a step towards the café but it's too late, he's striding towards us, face thunderous, white hair wild with rain.

'You,' he points a finger at me. 'What the hell d'you think you're doing, poking around, asking Reg about us? Haven't you done enough?'

This is the first time I've seen him since he was so rude to me at the letting agency, and now, in the face of his fury, all the well-worded arguments I've been storing in my head dry up.

'I was just asking a question about Enysyule,' I splutter, pulling myself together. 'Or can't I even do that?'

'Scavel-an-gow,' he spits, 'you're scheming with that Tremennor boy.'

'Oh? And what about you?' I snap. Liza takes my arm. I shake her off. 'Sabotaging my electricity, slapping me with made-up bills, trying your *best* to drive me out of town? Alexander is the only person who's been nice to me.'

'Ha! You're in league with them, I knew it.'

'In league with . . .? For god's sake you're paranoid!'

'Baint paranoid if it's true!'

The wind howls past the doorway, and for a moment we stare at each other in the rush of white noise. Roscarrow's face is crimson with anger. He opens his mouth to argue, but no words come out. He raises a shaking finger, points it at me again, before storming away into the wind. I let out a long breath, horrified to find tears welling in my eyes.

'God,' I mumble, swiping them away. 'What's his *problem*? He has no right to act like that.'

Liza grimaces. 'Sorry, Jess . . . he sort of does.'

'*What?*'

Liza looks miserable. 'I just mean, I think he has a right to be angry, after what Alex did.' She tries to straighten her ruined umbrella, before giving up. 'You have to admit, it was pretty low.'

Nausea twists through me. 'What do you mean? He didn't do anything, he had a word, that's all . . .' I trail off at the look on Liza's face. 'What? What is it?'

She gives a long sigh, dropping her head. 'I should've guessed he wouldn't tell you the truth,' she mumbles. 'All right, I don't know exactly what happened, just that Alex showed up at the boatyard the other day and . . .' She peers off into the rain.

'Tell me, please.'

'Apparently he got pretty nasty with Mel. Started threatening him with legal action, said he would start badmouthing the yard to all of Mel's clients unless he cooperated. I mean, everyone knows that the yard's been in financial trouble for a while now, and Mel can't afford to lose any business. I agree he was being difficult and uncooperative, but the way Alex handled it was . . .' she shrugs heavily. 'It was humiliating.'

I can't believe what I'm hearing, feel myself trembling with rage and the aftermath of the confrontation. Worse, I remember Jack's face, as I accused him of acting on some petty grudge.

'I didn't know.' Tears catch at the back of my throat. 'Alex said they'd just talked. I thought he was being kind.'

Liza's face softens. 'Kind to *you*,' she points out, 'not to them. I'm sorry, Jess. It's a long and very bitter history you've found yourself caught up in here.'

My fingers slip on the screen of the phone, wet with rain. I press it to my ear under the hood of my coat.

Pick up the phone, pick up damn it.

'Jess,' Alex answers, sounding puzzled. In the background, I can hear clinking, the low chatter of a restaurant. 'What's up? Can I call you back? I can't really talk now, we're just—'

'You lied, about what happened with Roscarrow.' I have to raise my voice, above a blast of freezing rain. 'You said you just talked to him!'

There's silence and for a minute I think I've lost signal. Then I hear a muffled curse, footsteps, as if Alex is taking the phone somewhere else.

'I *did* just talk to them,' he says, voice low. 'I told you.'

'Talking doesn't mean bullying,' I tell him furiously, 'it doesn't mean threatening their livelihood over something as petty as electricity.'

'And who told you this?' he says. 'I wonder, was it the Roscarrows?'

'No, it wasn't, and anyway, that's not the point. What the hell made you think you could do something like that on my behalf? No wonder they hate me!'

'Jess,' Alex sighs with frustration, 'you're new here, you don't know how it all works. Sometimes threats are the only thing their like will respond to.'

I stop dead on the leaf-clogged ground. 'Their *like*?'

'You know what I mean.'

'No, I don't.' I'm shaking with anger. 'Whatever snobbish issues you have with the Roscarrows, they're yours, not mine.'

'Look,' Alex snaps, 'if it wasn't for me you'd still be sitting in the dark, scribbling your little fairy stories—' He bites off the words, too late. 'I'm sorry,' he says, after a few tense breaths. 'I didn't mean that.'

In the silence that follows, I feel the rage ebbing away, leaving me sick and cold and empty. 'Yes you did,' I tell him.

'Jess, you're being ridiculous. Let's talk later, when you're less worked up.'

'No. I don't want to talk any more. I'm . . . I'm sorry, Alex. This was clearly a mistake.'

'But—'

I hang up. For a long while I just stare at the phone, smudged from my skin, the raindrops landing thick and fat on its surface. When it starts to ring again I turn it off, shove it into my pocket. The wind howls past, laden with rain. I've been so stupid. What's worse, I've been naïve. I deliberately ignored my common sense, my better judgement, and for what? A quick fix? A solution to my problems, no questions asked? Falling into the very preconceptions I've railed against in others . . .

By the time I reach the stone, I'm exhausted, just want to curl up and never see anyone again. I ignore the prickling at the back of my neck, and plough on, into the valley. At the cottage, the key is slick and cold in my fingers. I let myself in, only to discover that inside isn't much warmer than out, yesterday's fire dead in the grate. I start to light a new one, coaxing a flame from the damp kindling. It has almost caught when the wind howls through the rag-stuffed windows, down onto the hearth, smothering the fire before I can get it started. I grab the poker, try to bring it back to life, but there's no warmth, just dead ash and cold smoke.

There's a questioning sort of noise at my elbow, and I turn around to see Perrin, standing on the flagstones, dishevelled from the wind and rain. Sobbing, I gather him onto my lap and wrap my cardigan around him, hugging him for warmth and comfort. He doesn't protest, just bumps my chin with his damp head, until my tears subside and I can sit back, to stroke the last droplets of water from his fur.

'Everything's such a mess, Perrin,' I murmur, as the wind and the rain pummel the cottage. 'What am I going to do?'

* * *

What is time to a stone? What are tears? A fleeting drop of salt-water on a face that will soon be gone. And yet, every tear is a catalyst; every touch of lip or fingertip changes the world, in a tiny way, forever.

* * *

The storm rages. It tears at the thatch of the cottage, rips branches from the trees, leaving pale wounds on their trunks. It makes the high, old holly trees shake and shudder, like a beast convulsing. It drives sleet into the face of the young woman who battles through the night. Her fine gloves are soaked and useless, her fingers numb, and the wood is dark, all dark. The moon is behind cloud and when it does show it is no help, a thin scraping of tin in the black sky. The girl staggers on, her shoes stubbing against the cobbles.

But the valley is not silent, and although the cottage is tightly shuttered against the winter, light and noise spill from its cracks, voices, singing:

Canel ha jynjor gans clovys druth, ha dowr tom Frynk, a'm ros tron ruth!

Inside, six people are celebrating. They are salt-stained and dishevelled, as though they have been grappling with the waves. A man and a woman sit at the long table, laughing, while the others – men and boys all – jump to the music of a fiddle, kicking reeds about the floor. In the bread oven, buns are baking. They are gaudy with saffron, jewelled with currants, filling the cottage with the scent of stolen sugar and spice. Outside, the dark night presses and the cold threatens to squeeze life to its dregs, but in here, for now, all is relief and plenty.

Stacked about the room are barrels and boxes, sacks and crates, most still caked with wet sand. The woman's fingers are stained with ink as she tries to take an inventory through the raucous merriment:

Cinnamon, ginger, nutmegs and cloves and brandy gave me my jolly red nose!

The woman signals, and one of the men breaks off from the dance to lever the top from a small barrel. Liquid slops inside. The song falters, and no one moves or speaks as the woman dips a finger and places it in her mouth. They watch as she tastes, searching for the ruinous trace of salt water. When she smiles, and nods once, mirth returns to the room. Before the barrel can be re-sealed, cups are dipped, measures siphoned off and knocked down eager throats. The woman only shakes her head and goes back to her notation.

Outside, battered by the paws of the storm, the girl stumbles on. Her clothes were not made for such weather. The winter ground has ruined her thin boots – intended for floors cushioned by rugs – and the velvet of her dress sucks in the freezing rain and won't let go. Yet her face is grim and determined, for now she has a guide: a small, black shadow that is buffeted by the wind, running along the path before her, showing the way.

Finally, through the trees she sees a glimmer of light, hears a snatch of voices raised in song. She pushes on, slipping in the mud of the meadow, up to the cottage. She can smell the woodsmoke now, and the oil lamps, can almost feel the warmth, but cannot summon the strength to cry out. One foot gives under her as she steps onto the threshold, and she crumples.

The shadow resolves itself from the night, eyes flashing. It leaps over the girl onto the front step, scratching and yowling for the door to be opened. Sure enough, bolts are drawn back and light spills out, like beer from a cask. A man stands on the other side. He is tall and broad-shouldered, with a thick beard beneath weather-worn skin. His eyes are bright with drink and mirth; bright as the shell of a hazelnut.

When he sees the shape on the cold ground a curse falls from his mouth. The woman from the table appears beside him and stops dead, before rushing out into the storm. She calls to the man and he lifts the girl, carries her into the warmth of the cottage, though the sodden clothes double her weight.

The singing and merriment cease. All faces are turned to the girl, propped in a chair by the fire. Compared to them, she looks like spirit, pale and bloodless. One of the men mutters anxiously. The woman with the ink-stained fingers pays him no mind; she is busy untying the ribbons of the girl's cloak, stripping it off and wrapping a blanket in its place. Next, she tugs at the fingers of the sodden gloves. One flies free, lands on the flagstones.

The broad-shouldered man picks it up, smoothes the design embroidered onto the cuff. There is only one family in the area who could afford such costly workmanship; the same family whose name is stamped across the barrels and casks and crates that fill the cottage. The girl is coming to. She shudders and coughs, and the woman holds a glass of brandy to her lips. Its fire finds a way down her throat and she blinks her eyes open. She focuses on the woman before her. Slowly, recognition blooms.

'Mistress . . . Roscarrow?' she whispers.

The woman smiles a small, sad smile. 'Aye.' She pushes the wet hair from the girl's forehead, the way she used to, so many years ago.

'She can't stay here,' the man says, face hard. 'She's not welcome.'

'Enough,' the woman leans in towards the girl. 'Don't listen to him, cheel. What's happened? Why are you here?'

The girl's voice seems to come from a long way off.

'I lost the way.' She looks around the room blindly, before her eyes settle on a black shape, perched by the hearth. 'Your cat found me by the holly, he sang and sang until I followed. He isn't—?'

'Aye,' the woman says, 'the very same.'

'He must be an old man now.' The girl's eyes drift closed. The woman shakes her firmly.

'No, cheel. Tell us why you're here.'

The girl forces her eyes open again. Her cheeks, so pale before, are starting to flush. 'They are coming,' she says urgently. 'I heard them, in the hall. They know and are coming.'

'Who?' The woman's voice is calm. 'Tell us, quickly.'

'Papa, the customs men.' The girl shivers. 'The militia. I heard them talking, about what they will do, and I had to come. I thought if I ran here I might be in time, but I lost the way . . .'

The youngest boy cries in alarm. He is peering out of the gap between the shutters. There are bright points of light in the darkness, torches and lanterns, approaching fast. The room bursts into frenzy. Hands grasp weapons, try in vain to hide the goods that fill the place. Quick as a snake, the woman snatches up the paper from the table, filled with her writing, and throws it onto the fire. Her hands are still guilty with ink; she spits upon them and plunges them into a sack of flour that stands by the oven, the white powder hiding the stains.

The bearded man stands motionless, staring at the door. From outside comes the sound of hooves on hard ground, of creaking leather and voices shouting orders through the night.

'We're done,' he says.

In the chair by the fire, the girl closes her eyes. 'I'm sorry,' she whispers, tears on her cheeks.

'I'm sorry . . .' I murmur. There's a noise from somewhere near the floor, and Perrin leaps onto the bed. He's damp and muddy, leaves caught in his long fur.

'Urgh,' I protest, trying to keep him at arm's length, but he's determined to rub his cold, wet head against my face, purring and purring all the while.

'All right,' I tell him, 'all right.'

Morning greeting done, he settles down on my chest, allowing me to close my eyes and drowse for a while. I *don't* try to remember the dream, I know better by now. Instead, I let it wash over me, through me, filling me with its meaning. An old affection between two women, strong enough to sweep prejudice and names aside, for one of them to risk her life . . . I sigh and open my eyes. Compared to that, what I have to do seems simple.

Still, it's with a deep sense of nervousness that I get ready to leave the house. A cup of tea stands cold on the table. I haven't been able to drink it. I wrap up warm, trying to smother the trembling in my stomach with an extra jumper. I feed the fire to keep the house – and Perrin – warm. Just for a moment, through the woodsmoke, I think I catch a familiar scent. I peer into the huge fireplace, wincing at the heat, and sure enough, in the side of the flue there's a dark hole, clogged with dirt and old ash. A bread oven, I realise, one that once baked buns for a family, filled with stolen currants and saffron . . . My hand lingers at its edge.

Before I leave, I take Thomasina's sketchpad down from the dresser. Carefully, I wrap it in a tea towel and place it in my bag. And then there's nothing for it but to step through the front door, and face my decision.

Outside, the storm has abated, leaving a day that's strangely still and heavy. The ground is littered with broken twigs and branches, and the trees, which before were clinging to their last, tattered finery, have been stripped bare. In contrast, the holly grove around the stone looks magnificent, the leaves deep green and shining. Here and there, I can see berries ripening, turning red. Although my skin tingles as I pass through the clearing, today, my head remains clear. Perhaps the Perranstone can sense I have enough on my mind.

Just follow the stream to the river and you'll find us.

For a while, the water rushes busily alongside the old road, sweeping autumn debris downstream. Ferns line the bank, roots and rocks covered with moss so thick it looks like green velvet. Halfway to the village, the stream leaves the road behind, disappears towards the river. I hesitate at the fork in the path. What if this is a bad idea? *Stop being ridiculous*, I tell myself, *this is the only good idea you've had since coming here.*

Eventually, the path slopes downward, the earth changes from dark loam to grey river mud, and I find myself on the bank of a sheltered inlet, a secret cove, almost. I must have passed through the woods behind it a dozen times without knowing it was here. A couple of gulls fly past, squalling obscenities at each other. I wish I was one of them, so I could see this place as they do; river and wood, valley and stone. *Roscarrow and Tremennor and Enysyule between them.*

At the head of the inlet I can see a yard. Boats in various states of disrepair list in the mud or float gently in the shallows. There are flat-bottom barges and green-stained dinghies, tightly battened yachts and well-worn fishing boats. Everywhere there are piles of cable and rope, rusted metal fittings and old, faded buoys.

I pick my way through it all, towards a building that sprawls along the riverbank. The ground floor is made of stone, the same grey-weathered stone that forms the walls of Enysyule, but the rest is wood. Two stories rise, higgledy-piggledy, as though they've been constructed from offcuts and spare boards and scavenged window frames. There's even a porthole, overlooking the cove. I've never seen anywhere like it.

As I get closer, I hear a repetitive, scraping, clattering sound. On a slipway before the building I can see a figure in a woollen jumper, white hair crazing in the breeze. Mel Roscarrow. His head is turned away from me, and for a moment I almost lose my nerve, go creeping back to Enysyule.

'Unless you're here about a boat,' he says abruptly, 'you can save your breath. I don't have time to stand around being bamfered.'

I force myself to take a deep breath, to stay calm.

'I'm not here about a boat.' I move forward until I can sit on the slipway wall. 'And I don't know what bamfering is but I'm pretty sure I'm not here for that either.'

He still hasn't turned around, fussing with what looks like a paint scraper.

'I'm here to apologise,' I say awkwardly.

Mel Roscarrow doesn't reply, only goes back to what he was doing, scraping barnacles from the side of a boat.

'I'm sorry for the other day,' I carry on, louder. 'And for what Alexander said to you. He lied to me, if that makes any difference. If I'd known, I never would have—' I stop, cheeks burning. Mel Roscarrow shakes a stubborn barnacle from the end of the scraper.

'And Enysyule,' he rumbles. 'I suppose you're sorry you ever laid eyes on it?'

'No, I'm not,' I say indignantly, before I can stop myself. 'I love it there. I'm sorry that *you* feel hard done by. That's really nothing to do with me, though you've tried your best to make me feel guilty for it.' I stop. Mel Roscarrow has turned around and is smiling. A small, bitter smile, but a smile none-theless. I swallow. No sense stopping now. 'And your wager,' I tell him, 'was stupid and hurtful.'

He narrows his eyes at me. They're darker than Jack's, deep brown in his wrinkled face. 'Yes,' he says eventually, 'suppose it was. Suppose I'm sorry for it.'

I can tell it's as much of an apology as I'm going to get; though, I remind myself, *his* apology was not what I came for. After a tense pause, we both start speaking at once.

'Listen, I've brought—'

'Was about to make—'

We stop, waiting for the other to go first.

'You—' we both say.

'Oh bugger it,' he throws down the scraper. 'I'm making tea. Come in if you want some.'

The entire ground floor of the house is given over to boats, but the upper floor forms a wide, open space, where a kitchen has been built into one corner, a sort of living room into another, filled with squashy, worn armchairs and mismatched bookshelves. A wood-burning stove heats the place, fed by scraps and offcuts from the yard below. Mel chucks another few lumps of wood inside and checks the kettle that stands on its top.

'Always hot this way,' he mutters, fetching a teapot.

'Do you live here?' I ask, looking around.

'Aye,' he points to the river with a teaspoon. 'Though I sleep on my boat out front. Don't sleep well on land. Jack lives up here, mostly.'

While he bustles, fetching milk and biscuits, I wander over to the window. The view across the cove is fantastic, even in this dull weather. No other houses, just the glassy water and the reflections of trees. River and land in all its changing seasons. No wonder they're afraid of losing it.

'This is a beautiful place,' I say quietly, almost to myself.

''Tis,' Mel comes to stand beside me. 'This river's in our blood.'

All at once I remember my dream, a family in the cottage, five men and one woman, the river in *their* blood too. A shudder passes over me.

Mel notices. 'Someone walk over your grave?' he asks, pulling out a chair at the table.

I don't answer. *Does this happen to everyone who stays at Enysyule?* I wonder, as I take a seat opposite him. *Do they see things? Dream things, the way I do?* Impossible to ask, without sounding crazy. Instead, I open my bag.

'I . . . Jack told me that Enysyule means a lot to you.' I unwrap the sketchpad and place it on the table in front of him. 'I found this in the cottage. I know it isn't really mine to give, but I thought you might like to keep it.'

I watch his face as he opens the cover, trying to decipher his expression. He turns the pages, taking in the different sketched views of Enysyule, a corner of its thatch, a patch of blackberries, heavy with fruit, the meadow, full of sunlight.

'That's my favourite,' I say, leaning forward when he reaches the drawing of the cat-being, made of smoke. 'Your aunt must have had a wonderful imagination. I can tell it's meant to be Perrin, look at the eyes.'

I glance up to find him watching me intently. After a while, he sets the sketchbook aside, folds weathered hands around his mug.

'What do you know about Enysyule, Miss Pike?' he asks, his lined face serious.

I take a sip of tea, feeling like I'm being tested.

'It's an old place,' I say, wincing at how simplistic that sounds. 'It's been there for a long time, the cottage.' My eyes fall on the sketchpad. 'Before the cottage was the road, and before the road, before anything was built, there was the stone. It has always been there, stone and holly, marking the boundary of the valley—' I stop, embarrassed, unnerved by the words that seem to have bypassed my thoughts to fall straight from my lips. Mel is watching me closely.

'How do you know that?' he asks. 'About the road and the stone?'

'I can't remember,' I say, hurriedly taking a biscuit as a distraction. 'Michaela must have mentioned it.'

He watches me for a moment longer before his face softens.

'Yes,' he says, 'that must be it.' He swigs his own tea. 'So, Miss Pike. Humour an old man, tell me how you ended up in these parts. *Your* version, not the gossip.'

I don't know whether it's the relief, or the simple act of sitting across a kitchen table from someone, drinking tea, but I find myself telling him everything. About how my dreams of becoming a writer came true, only to lead to my breakup. About how I stumbled across the advert for the cottage on the very day it went live; about how, within an hour of seeing it, I was boarding a train, speeding west, driven by nothing more than instinct.

'I didn't intend to sign anything that day,' I admit. 'Then you were there, and when you said I wouldn't last a night at Enysyule, I sort of . . . snapped.'

Across the table, Mel shifts uncomfortably. 'Well. Looks like it might have worked out all right.'

I smile and eventually his mouth twitches in response.

'Better get back to work,' he says briskly. 'Thanks for Thomasina's sketches, Miss Pike. And for coming here.'

He holds out a hand. It's only when I shake it that I realise how gnarled his fingers are, knotted with arthritis. As we walk downstairs, he flexes them painfully. Outside, the barnacle-encrusted boat stands waiting.

'Is that difficult?' I ask, as he picks up the scraper, wondering if he'll see straight through me. 'Chipping those things off?'

'Baint difficult,' he grunts. 'Just dull. Why? You planning on being a yard hand?'

'Can I try?' I drop my bag on the slipway.

'It's a messy job,' Mel warns, eyeing my raincoat.

'That's all right.' I take the scraper. 'So, I just—' I dig the scraper into a cluster of barnacles, showering myself with bits of shell. 'Urgh.'

Mel barks a laugh. 'No, look, do it in one motion, like this,' a rain of barnacles falls to the floor. 'Got it?'

He fetches another scraper, and soon we're working alongside each other in silence, broken only by the rasp and rattle of shells. The smell of old seawater and river mud rises up around us. It brings back another flash of my dream: of salt-stained casks and men with sand on their boots.

'Mel,' I ask, 'was there ever any smuggling around here?'

'Smuggling? I'd say so.'

'I mean right here, on the river and at Enysyule?'

'Course,' he carries on working, 'were a way of life. Folk didn't have any choice. They'd have starved otherwise.' He looks over with a grin. 'They used to paint their boats black, black sides, black sails, so as they wouldn't be seen. And when they brought the goods inland, they'd soap up their horses, so that if they were caught, customs men wouldn't be able to get a grip.' He mimes grappling with a slippery horse, and I find myself laughing. 'We Roscarrows were a pretty lively bunch at it, as I understand.'

'Were they ever caught?' I ask, scraping away again so that he doesn't see the interest on my face. 'Your ancestors?'

Hooves in the darkness, panic in the cottage, a girl with tears on her face, her warning come too late . . .

'They were,' Mel says matter-of-factly. 'My granddad reckoned near enough the whole family swung for it, save the widow and the youngest. They got kicked off their land, came to live here.' He jerks his head at the jumble of buildings behind us. 'Give you one guess who claimed Enysyule after that.'

I don't need to answer, but he's waiting for me to. 'The Tremennors?'

'Aye, the bloody Tremennors. Why d'you want to know about all this, anyway?'

I hesitate, wondering whether to risk telling the truth. 'I've been having these—'

From the corner of my eye, I see movement and straighten up, banging my head on the boat. Jack Roscarrow stands at the top of the slipway, staring down at us with undisguised confusion. Mel follows my gaze.

'Afternoon, lad,' he calls.

I wonder how long he's been standing there, how much he's heard. I push the hair off my face, feeling clumsy and disoriented.

'Hello, Jack,' I say.

He still doesn't answer, looking from one of us to the other.

'Miss Pike and I have been straightening a few things out,' Mel says cheerfully. I think he's *enjoying* this. 'Why don't you go and make us another round of tea?'

Jack meets my eyes, only to look away hurriedly. 'Just came to get the van,' he mutters. 'Have to pick up that paint before the depot closes.'

'Depot doesn't close for two hours,' Mel calls but Jack's already hurrying away into one of the sheds. After a while, the sound of an engine starting drifts towards us.

I let out a sigh.

'Ah, don't mind him,' says Mel, scratching his stubble. 'He's always been a stubborn old weasel.'

* * *

Although humans fight for land, land itself can never fight back. It has no fists to raise in anger, feels no bravery or fear. Its best defence is to be forgotten, or better still, to be remembered by only a few ...

* * *

That day marks the start of new decisions. More than ever, I'm determined to make a place for myself here. But what can I offer Lanford, apart from gossip? I can't build or mend things with my hands, like Mel and Jack. I can't work the land, or watch for wrecks, or draw like Thomasina Roscarrow once did.

'I don't even know how to make blackberry wine,' I tell my mother over the phone, a few days later. 'All I have is my writing. And that doesn't make sense half the time.'

'Jessamine,' comes her sharp reply, and I know that I'm about to receive a talking-to. 'When I first arrived in this country, I thought the same. I thought, "they will never accept me, there is no space in their world for me." I was wrong, and now, so are you.'

She is walking somewhere, the distant sounds of London filling the spaces between her words. I press the phone closer to my ear, missing her desperately.

'You have *yourself*,' she says firmly, 'you have everything that you are to share with these people. You have new eyes and a fresh mind to see the things they cannot.'

I blink back tears, her words enveloping me, like the sun on a cool spring day. 'Thanks, Mama.'

'And if they cannot appreciate you, then you should give up and come home.'

Her indignation makes me laugh. 'I am not giving up!' I tell her. 'I love it here. When you see it you'll understand.'

She makes a noise in return. 'And are you eating properly?'

'Yes,' I say, thinking of the pantry, stacked with tins. 'I can cook for myself, you know.'

'Beans on toast is not cooking, Jessamine.' She sighs. 'Do you even have an oven? Or will I be cooking the turkey over the fire, like a man in a cave?'

At first I think I've misheard. I hold the phone tighter. 'You'll come here for the holidays?' I ask. 'You mean it?'

My mother laughs her impatient laugh. 'It is important to you so ... yes, we will come. I have told your sister and Michael that is the plan. You have enough space for us?'

'Of course!' I'm grinning with excitement. 'Although whoever takes my bed might have to share with Perrin.'

'Perr-in?' my mother pronounces slowly. 'This is the cat you must look after?'

'Yes, I can't wait for you to meet him.'

She laughs drily. 'You talk like he is a person.'

I almost leap back down the lane towards the cottage. *Christmas at Enysyule*, I tell myself, stepping inside. Mum never celebrated it growing up. It wasn't until she married my dad that she started to go along with traditional holiday things. Dad *loved* Christmas, like a kid. He always insisted on a huge tree, decorations, turkey, carols, everything. When he died, she tried to keep it all up, for our sake, though it was never the same without him. Once we got a bit older, we realised how much Christmas made her miss him, so we decided to keep things quieter. For the past ten years, we've mostly ignored it.

But now, it feels *right*, to have Christmas here. It'll be a tight squeeze, to fit my mum and my sister and my brother-in-law in, but this house should be full of people at the Yuletide, I know it. Perrin is curled up in a tight ball by the hearth, his paw over his eyes.

'Perrin!' I announce, waking him up. 'My family are coming to visit!' I ruffle his stomach, imagining this place on Christmas Eve: holly branches decorating the mantelpiece, hung with colourful ornaments, a cosy log fire and the smell of warm spices. Perrin makes a noise and looks out at me from under his paw. *Was that worth waking me up for?* his expression seems to say.

I sigh, looking around at the reality of the cottage: crumbling plaster that still needs patching, window frames that still need fixing, stone that still needs scrubbing.

'We have a lot to do before this place is presentable,' I tell him.

Worst of all is the plumbing. It clanks and howls like a ghoul every time I turn a tap. Surely, now that Mel and I have resolved our differences, it'll be easier to find a plumber? And there was that handywoman Reg told me about. I've asked Michaela about hiring her, but she and Liza have been strangely non-committal.

'Perhaps she thinks I'm not going to stay here,' I murmur to Perrin. 'Perhaps she thinks I'm going to leave, after what happened with Alex. I'll have to go and correct her, won't I?'

Perrin makes a noise and buries his head under his paw, no intention of giving up his warm seat by the fire for the chill, misty day outside. So, I go alone. My heart beats steadily as I walk the valley, warming my blood, even as my nose and fingers turn numb with cold. I'm so lost in thought that I reach the clearing long before I expect to.

Even after almost a month, I'm still not used to the stone. Does it have this effect on everyone? Rather than hurrying past as usual, I stop to examine it. The surface is wet, gleaming in the muted afternoon light. I take a step closer, another, as close as I dare before I look up. There, just above my ear is a mark, a gouge, where something has struck the stone and chipped it away, like a ball from a flintlock pistol. Again, I hear the shot, thundering across the clearing, I hear the sound of laboured breathing as a young woman staggers through a storm, I hear a horse's cry and the creak of boots on snow . . .

I pull back. The stone stands over me, sightless, like the cataract-filmed eye of something very, very old. Before I have a chance to think about what I'm doing, I'm bending down to look through the hole in its middle. It frames a view of the path on the other side. Today it looks different; something has changed. The undergrowth looks flattened, several holly branches have been snapped, bent at awkward angles, as though someone has shoved them roughly aside. Below, driven into the earth is a sign, made from bright, new wood and sharp-edged plastic. The wrongness of it jars so forcefully that for a few seconds, I can't even take in the words:

PRIVATE LAND
PROPERTY OF TREMENNOR ESTATES
TRESPASSERS WILL BE PROSECUTED

I throw the phone down on Michaela's desk, sending pens skittering to the floor.

'What's this?' I demand, hands trembling with anger.

On the screen, there's a photo of the sign in the clearing, large and inescapable. She stares at it silently, and after a moment Liza comes out of the back room, two mugs in hand.

'What if we—?' she stops dead when she sees me. Her eyes take in my furious expression, my hands, muddy from dragging the sign out of the ground. She obviously knows exactly what's going on. They both do.

'Are you going to explain?' I demand into the silence.

Michaela sighs, hands the phone back to me. She's changed since I last saw her, somehow deflated, bags under her eyes, her ordinarily perfect hair hastily scraped back.

'I was about to telephone you, Jess, to ask you to come in for a discussion.' She looks up at me at last. 'Roger Tremennor has . . . taken issue with the situation at Enysyule.'

'What? *How* can he take issue with it? The lease is signed.'

'It isn't the lease he's disputing,' Liza says, setting a mug down in front of Michaela. 'It's ownership of the whole valley. He's claiming that the Roscarrows never actually owned the land; that they were only tenants of the Tremennors, under some centuries-old agreement between the two families.'

'That's ridiculous,' I burst, yet even as I say it, I hear Mel's voice again: *give you one guess who claimed Enysyule after that.* 'Is there any proof of this "agreement"?' I ask tautly.

'Yes,' Michaela rubs at her forehead. 'Apparently Thomasina signed something before she died, acknowledging that the land wasn't hers.' She takes a large gulp from the mug and winces. 'What is this?'

'Double G&T,' Liza says. 'Thought you needed it.'

Michaela nods sombrely and takes another sip. 'I don't understand it,' she mutters. 'Thomasina didn't mention anything like this when she asked us to administrate Enysyule. Unless she really was, you know.' She flutters a hand around her head. 'I mean she *did* try to leave it all to Perrin—'

'Michaela,' Liza interrupts, casting a worried look at me. 'You know that's not what this is all about.'

I stand in front of them, anger ebbing away, leaving me helpless. I've been waiting for this, I realise, ever since the night of the Allantide party.

'What does this mean for me?' I ask. 'For Enysyule?'

Michaela shrugs. 'I'm not sure. I'm sorry, Jess, it's an odd situation. The way the cottage is managed is unorthodox. It's part of a trust fund, set up to provide a caretaker for the property for the duration of Perrin's life. I mean, that's complicated enough.' She tails off, takes another sip of gin.

'But it's all legal?' There's something furtive in her manner that I don't like.

'Yes,' Liza draws out the word. 'Technically.'

'*Technically?*'

'A court could challenge it,' Michaela says heavily. 'Which is exactly what Roger's threatening to do.' She looks up at me, face drawn. 'We've had a letter from his solicitor. He's proposed a meeting between all parties, to discuss the situation. It doesn't look good. It's clear he wants the land, and if he has proof . . .' She shakes her head, staring around at the tiny, cluttered office. 'We're a small business, Jess. There's no way we'll be able to absorb the cost of court proceedings.'

I close my eyes, squeeze them tight, trying to take the information in. Is she saying that I'll have to leave Enysyule, now, when I am just starting to learn its ways? *And Perrin?* I want to ask, *and my dreams? And the land? And the stone?*

'When is this meeting?' I force myself to say instead.

'First thing next week.' Liza goes to her desk, picks up a piece of paper lying there. 'Here, we're supposed to pass this on to you.'

I glance at it briefly. A scary, officially worded letter where I'm referred to only as 'the tenant'. I screw it into a ball. 'Nothing's certain yet?' I ask them. 'Enysyule is still leased to me?'

They exchange a glance.

'Yes,' says Michaela. 'For now.'

I almost call Alex a dozen times before I get back to the cottage, to the safety of NO SIGNAL. I want to rage at someone, I want him to apologise, say that he'll talk to his father. *That's not how this works*, I tell myself, keeping the phone firmly zipped in my pocket. I don't need any more of his 'favours'. If I'm the caretaker of Enysyule, then it's my job to keep it safe. All of it.

I wish Thomasina had left me something, instructions, a letter, a note, anything to tell me what to do. I've searched the cottage top to bottom and found nothing. I've looked everywhere, except for in the locked trunk at the foot of the bed. I've never been able to find a key for it, and Michaela has no record of one. I can't shake the feeling something important is waiting for me there.

As it is, the most personal items I've found are Thomasina's sketchbook, her handwriting on a few bottles of blackberry wine, her doodles on a newspaper article— The thought stops me in the doorway of the cottage. The article. What did it say? Something about Roger Tremennor and plans . . .?

Perrin looks up, meows at me as I hurry past, taking the stairs two at a time. I shunt open the door to the spare room, praying that I didn't throw the newspaper away. It's not on the table. What did I do with it? Frantically I hunt about the floor, pulling at dustsheets that haven't been moved for years, shoving boxes aside, disturbing spiders and woodlice. *Please say I didn't burn it, please . . .*

Perrin strolls in, intrigued by the noise and the chaos. From the corner of my eye I see him bat lazily at a woodlouse as it scuttles past, before making a beeline for the armchair by the window. The seat of it rustles as he jumps up. I look around to find him making himself comfortable on the folded newspaper.

Heart thudding, I coax it out from underneath him. I'd forgotten all about the article. Now, in the picture I recognise Roger Tremennor, even without his Allantide costume and make-up. He stands on the steps of the manor, arms folded, looking down into the camera. Thomasina's doodles remain; at some point before she died she must have inked the devil horns onto his head, the tusks that sprout from his lips, a pointy tail, flies buzzing around him. I'd laugh if I wasn't so distracted by the title of the article:

TREMENNOR SUBMITS MARINA PLANS

Roger Tremennor – of Tremennor Estates – has today announced his intention to spearhead the development of a multi-million-pound marina complex, on the banks of the Lan, near the village of Lanford.

'This area is crying out for modernisation,' Tremennor said in a recent interview. 'A marina complex will not only attract international tourism, but boost the local economy, providing jobs and amenities for residents and visitors alike.'

Tremennor has already faced stiff opposition from regional wildlife groups, who protest that the presence of a large-scale marina on the river will disrupt its unique and delicate ecosystem. Last year, after negotiations with the district council, Tremennor acquired a strip of undeveloped riverbank, in a deal that has been called into question by some local residents. While the land itself is only a fraction of what would be required for a marina site, Tremennor states that he is 'confident' additional land will be found in due course. More information on the 'planning' section of the Lanford Town Council website.

I stare down at Tremennor's graffitied face. No wonder he's trying to pounce on Enysyule. A whole valley, so near the river . . . He must have had his eye on it for years. Abruptly I remember what Alex said, the last morning we were together. *I've got to go and meet Dad and some investors about this new marina thing.*

He knew, I realise. Even when we were together, he knew what his father was planning, and said nothing. The thought of developers and investors tramping through the valley in suits and hard hats makes me feel physically ill, let alone the idea that the cottage might be knocked down, the Perranstone fenced off or 'relocated', the old road torn up . . . And what would happen to Perrin? I can't imagine him living anywhere else. He wouldn't survive.

'Tremennor's lying,' I murmur. It helps to say it aloud. 'Thomasina was a *Roscarrow*, she'd never sign the land over to him.' Perrin looks back at me, with his wise yellow eyes. 'We just have to prove it somehow,' I say, touching the soft fur of his head. 'We have to.'

★   ★   ★

Forgotten, the land returns to its wildness. It grows claws of brambles and briars, nettles that sting, roots that trip, grass that hides a hundred places to turn an ankle or lame a leg. Like a child forsaken, it becomes hard and unruly, and will not respond to the hand that tries to beat the wildness from it. Better to leave it savage than try to tame it that way. Better to leave it forgotten.

★   ★   ★

I can't write. Not now, when there's so much to think about, so much at stake. Instead, I search the house over again, looking for a key for the trunk. *What if there are land deeds in there?* I think, rooting through the dresser drawers. *There could be paperwork, a Will, a letter, anything . . .*

Nothing. I find myself sitting before the trunk, tracing its pattern with my fingertips. The wood is carved all over, roughly, as though someone had the vision but not the skill to realise it. An abstract design; swirls that stretch from edge to edge. In the centre, two knots look out from the wood like eyes. I sit with my back against the wall, and return the inhuman stare it gives me.

'Help me,' I whisper, to the cottage, the valley, to anything that might be listening. 'You've shown me things before. Please, show me something that will help.' Slowly, deliberately, I close my eyes, and let my thoughts slip.

I stare at the blackness behind my eyelids, broken only by half-imagined patterns of light. Minutes pass. My back aches from sitting on the bare floor, my legs are stiff. Just as I'm about to give up, stretch my limbs and open my eyes, I realise that they're already open. The pale, swirling shapes that fill my vision are snowflakes. The blackness all around is that of night; the stiffness in my limbs is from the cold, the ache in my back from a long day, labouring on the near-frozen river.

Every step brings the creak of snow. With each footfall I walk away from myself, until I am not me, but a man, wrapped in a coat that has seen many winters. Although the snow ahead looks smooth as cotton, beneath there are burrows and hollows that can take a leg and snap it in two. The man grimaces and opens his jaw, cracking away the ice that has formed in his beard. There is a flask in his pocket. His eyes flood at the burn of the liquor, warming his throat enough to sing:

'*Ha'n kelynn yw an kynsa a'n gwydh oll y'n koes . . .*'

His cautious steps take him further into the valley. He did not want to come in here, not tonight, but the holly grove by the stone was silent and empty, and he has a promise to keep. The snow swarms in the lantern's beam, hypnotic; it threatens to make his eyes droop with tiredness. He widens them against the cold, sings again, and louder.

'*Kelynn! Kelynn!*'

Nothing will harm him, he reminds himself. The valley is in his blood. Still, that is hard to remember when the place has lain silent for so long, when even the owls are voiceless with cold. Folk in the village say the valley is haunted, home to buccas and spirits and the ghosts of his ancestors, put to death . . .

Something cracks beneath his boot and he swallows a cry of fright. He swings the lantern beam through the darkness, black as goat hide. He shudders and looks down, scuffs at the snow with his foot. Beneath is ice, the water of the ford trapped in glass. He steps onto it, tests his weight. He is close then. He holds the lantern high and strides on, through the falling snow.

Finally his light catches on the wall of the cottage garden, its surface piled with snow. His steps quicken, the ground easier here where there was once a path, and soon he sees a threshold, a door, dark with time. He stops, one gloved hand on its latch. Something has been here recently, scuffed the snow away from the step. He considers throwing his bag down and hurrying away, back towards the river. But he cannot. He has promised. It is his duty, as it was his father's, and his grandmother's before. He sucks some of the ice from his beard and pushes open the door.

'*Hou*?' he calls, voice cracking. 'Perrin?'

Something shifts in the darkness. Something large and human-shaped. Terrified, the man recoils.

'Who's there?' a voice calls.

The lantern trembles in his hand as he raises it, shines it into the ruined cottage. There, by the empty hearth he sees a face, pale as marble, a pair of eyes, an open mouth.

'*Piw os ta*?' he demands. He starts to cross himself, changes his mind. It would make no difference, here.

'Speak English, can't you?' the face says, and with that, the man's fear dissolves. He looks closer. The man in the cottage sits hunched against the wall, a greatcoat wrapped around him, hat pulled low on his head. A beard frames his chin, full of frost.

The man from the wood curses aloud. 'What are you doing here?'

'What does it look like?' the man by the hearth says. 'Freezing to death.' His hands close protectively around one leg. 'Horse threw me, by that damned stone. All I could do to crawl.' His anger is laced with fear. 'I've been here for hours. If you're the search party, you took your damn time.'

The man with the lantern turns, shining its light into the rest of the cottage. It looks empty. Snow has drifted across the floor, blown in through the broken windows. The only piece of furniture still whole is the huge kitchen table. Its surface glitters with frost, white and gold.

'I'm not the search party,' he says.

'Then what are you doing, skulking about? This is private land.' His eyes fall on the bag the man carries on his back. 'Poaching? I could have you jailed.' He shifts uncomfortably on the stones. 'I shall overlook it, if you'll assist me.'

'Not poaching,' the man says, placing the lantern on the cracked stone floor, sliding the bag from his back. 'I'm here to feed himself.'

'What are you talking about? There's no one here. Hasn't been for years.'

The man from the wood doesn't answer, only takes a number of newspaper-wrapped packages from his bag. The smell of roasted meat and fresh fish rises into the icy air of the cottage.

'Thank the Lord,' the man by the hearth says. He lunges for the food, but the man with the lantern drags it away, out of his reach.

'It's not for 'ee,' he tells him.

The other man's face contorts. 'Damn you.' He tries to heave himself forward only to fall back again, swearing, grasping at his leg. 'Don't try me. I know who you are, you're one of those river devils—'

'Melchizedek Roscarrow, I am.'

'I knew it.' The man slumps back, face twisted. 'What kind of heathen name is Melchizedek?'

'A bible name. What kind of name is "Godfyld"?'

'A family name.' He pauses. 'You know me, then?'

'Aye.'

'So, you will help me.' A tremor has crept into the man's voice. 'You will take me back to the manor.'

Before the man with the lantern can answer, there's a creak, a scuffling noise and he holds up his hand for silence. One breath becomes two, becomes three, until slowly, a shadow separates itself from the rest, prowls closer to the very edge of the lantern's beam.

Yellow eyes flash in the darkness. Yellow as tallow, yellow as corn, old eyes, wild as a hawk's.

'*Hou*, Perrin,' the man with the lantern whispers, and nudges one of the open packets of food forwards. Inch by inch, the cat eases itself closer to the food, nose twitching, eyes fixed on the two men. Its body is thin and rangy, long black fur matted in clumps, snow clinging to its paws. It growls low in its throat when the man tries to move.

'Here, Perrin,' he soothes. 'Here.' He reaches out, but the cat hisses and swipes, drawing blood from his fingers. As soon as he sits back, it snatches the fish, drags it off under the table. There is a strangled laugh from the fireplace.

'You came out here in a snowstorm to feed that flea-bitten thing?' The man in the greatcoat laughs again, a harsh sound, tinged by pain. 'I know I should be grateful for your foolishness—'

'Wudden expect you to understand,' the man with the lantern interrupts, unwrapping the rest of the food. From beneath the table comes the sound of teeth tearing at the fish, ravenous.

'It scratched you,' the man in the greatcoat says, trying to find warmth in his spite. 'I call that ungrateful. Beast looks half dead to me. If I had my gun here I'd shoot it and call it mercy.'

Before he can draw another breath, the man with the lantern is on him, seizing a fistful of his coat, dragging him up onto his injured leg.

'Don't say that,' he spits. 'Don't *ever* say that. Understand?' He shakes him hard, knocking his hat to the ground. 'Well?'

'Yes,' the man in the greatcoat gasps. 'Yes, I understand. Now please—'

The man with the lantern drops him to the floor, ignoring the cries of pain. He looks again at the shadows under the table, at the flash of tooth as the cat bolts its meal.

'If he's wild,' he says, 'it's your doing, and no one else's.' The anger leaves him as he gazes about. 'Can't blame him for going savage when his home is treated thus.'

'This is my land,' the man in the coat wheezes. 'I shall do with it as I like.'

'It's only your cruelty keeps it like this,' the man says. 'Else there'd be folks living here now, looking after it, like all your other tenants.' He opens the bag again. Outside, the snow falls, gentle and deadly. 'Perhaps my lot would be living here still,' he says.

With no reply from the squire, the man gets on with business. From the bag he takes a sheepskin, warm and soft, and an old blanket. He tucks them into a sheltered corner, like a bed. From his pocket he brings a paper-wrapped bundle of dried fish. He sets it on the mantelpiece, where an agile creature might leap to find it. That done, he slowly approaches the cat beneath the table. It has finished the fish, started on the chicken.

'We've not forgotten you,' he whispers. The cat ducks away when he tries to touch its fur, regards him suspiciously, with eyes that once closed in happiness as a human hand smoothed his back. Not now. Not any more.

With a sigh, the man straightens up, slings the empty bag over his shoulder. The man in the greatcoat watches silently, his lips turning blue. The man with the lantern takes out the flask once more, drinks long.

'I shall help,' he says, wiping his lips. 'I'll take you out of the valley, back to the manor, and not say one word of it.' He looks down at the injured man. 'In return, *you* make this place sound. Walls, windows, roof. And you'll give us leave to come here whenever we will, to feed himself.'

The man in the greatcoat shudders with pain and cold. 'Why not ask for money,' he says bitterly, 'or goods or land? I'd give it, whatever it was, I'd have to.'

'Eggs and oaths are easily broken,' the man with the lantern says shortly. He crosses the few steps, holds out a hand to the squire. 'Do we have an understanding?'

The man in the greatcoat opens his mouth, but no voice comes out, only a scratching, scraping sound, like something clawing at wood. I jerk back in alarm, slamming my head on the wall behind me, and open my eyes. Bedroom floor, fire glowing in the grate, just as I left it. The scraping, scratching noise starts up again, and I look around to find Perrin, sharpening his claws on the old wooden trunk.

'Perrin!' I burst, and he stops, one paw raised. His eyes are the same as the half-wild creature's, living alone in a ruined house. 'Perrin,' I say gently, and reach out to stroke his head.

For a moment, he's still under my hand, as though he too remembers a different time when he ran savage. Then he rubs his face on my palm, pads over and climbs into my lap. And although my legs have gone to sleep from sitting on the floor, I let him settle down. He purrs, kneading the sleeve of my jumper and I stroke away the wildness, trying to tell him without words that no matter what happens, he won't be abandoned, not this time.

*   *   *

The dream stays with me the next day as I walk through the valley on my way to see Mel. I'm not sure what I was hoping for last night; even if I had seen something that might help me fight for Enysyule, how would I explain it to anyone? *I saw it in a dream after staring at a wooden box,* I see myself telling a solicitor, who nods thoughtfully and writes *tenant is batshit crazy* in his notes.

I'm starting to realise that Enysyule is a place built on forgotten stories, scraps of memories, echoed moments both tiny and earth-shattering. But right now, what I need is something solid. I need ink on paper, a language that the law will understand. I'm wracking my brain so intently for ideas that I don't initially take any notice of the sound echoing through the valley. It's only when I near the stone that it fully registers; a dull repetitive thudding, like someone hammering. I stop dead on the path.

'Don't you dare,' I murmur under my breath, breaking into a run. 'Don't you bloody dare . . .'

When I stagger to a halt at the edge of the clearing a few minutes later, a cry of frustration escapes me. The sign is back, in exactly the same place as yesterday. Even worse, there's now another one, driven into the ground on the opposite site. Whoever put them there must have scarpered when they heard me coming; the feeling of another person lingers in the chill air, along with the smell of fresh wood.

I barely notice the stone's presence beneath my anger. This time, I don't hesitate. I slam my boot into the post, kicking it again and again until the sign begins to lean, until I can reach down and drag it out of the ground. A splinter catches the skin of my wrist, drawing blood, but I don't care. The second sign is hammered in more firmly, and I swear at it, dragging it to and fro until it comes free. I throw it down, panting triumphantly.

Only then do I feel a spark of pain, a trickle of wetness as blood wells from the graze on my wrist. Before I can inspect it, frantic barking splits the quiet of the wood, and a brown shape streaks out of the trees. My stomach flips with a horrible sense of déjà vu. It's Maggie. She recognises me, yapping and leaping at the boundary of the clearing without daring to cross. I can only stare at her, numb, when I realise who has been here, who is responsible for the signs.

A whistle echoes through the bare trees.

'Maggie?'

I swallow nausea, knowing what is about to happen.

'Maggie, come—' Alex sees me, and stops dead.

It's the first time we've been face to face since I broke things off. For an instant, I feel a flare of the old attraction, and guilt. Then I notice the toolbag in his hand, the mallet over his shoulder, and my anger returns, stronger than ever.

'Jess,' Alex says, his eyes travelling over my flushed face, my muddied hands. 'Hey, you're bleeding—' Something in my face prevents him from coming any closer. He lets the mallet fall to his side, as if I won't see it there. 'How did you hurt yourself?' he says awkwardly.

The signs lie broken at my feet. 'How d'you think?'

His face flames. 'You shouldn't do that. It'll only make things worse.'

'Worse than your father bullying me out of my home, so he can steal this land for his bloody marina?'

As soon as I mention the marina, Alex's jaw tightens. *He knew about it all along,* I remind myself. *All that talk of being glad I got Enysyule instead of his father was bullshit.*

'This—' He clears his throat. 'This has nothing to do with you. It's a local matter. And you're just a tenant, so . . .' He looks at me, a pleading look creeping across his face. 'I don't understand, Jess. How can this dump mean anything to you? You don't belong here.'

For a second, I'm so furious I can't speak. 'And where do I belong? London? Somewhere less *inconvenient* for you?' He opens his mouth to reply, shuts it rapidly as I take a step forwards. 'What the hell did you think would happen between us, Alex? How did you think I would react to all this? Shrug and accept an invitation to dinner?'

'I thought—'

'You thought what?'

'I thought it would work out,' he says, half-defiant, half-beseeching. 'I thought Dad would be doing you a favour, getting you out of that contract.'

'What, so I'd be forced to leave,' I spit, 'to go back where I came from?'

'No! I thought you could maybe . . . come and stay at mine instead.'

His words hang between us, like leaves frozen mid-fall. Maggie shuffles and whines, the emotions clear even to her. I can't respond, trembling with disbelief and contempt. I turn away and grab the signs.

'I can't let you take those—' Alex starts, but I shove past him, walk away into the wood without a word.

Mel Roscarrow shuffles about the kitchen, setting down a roll of kitchen paper, searching through the cupboards.

'It's fine, it's only a scratch,' I call as he hurries into the bathroom. Through the door I catch a glimpse of a claw-footed bath, an old sink set into a plank of wood.

'Even so.' He emerges with an ancient-looking bottle in his hand. 'Iodine,' he tells me, wrestling off the lid. 'Nothing like it.'

I don't have the energy to protest as he starts to soak a piece of kitchen towel in the stuff. The confrontation with Alex has left me weak and shaky.

'Give,' Mel orders, and I hold out my wrist, pulling back my sleeve so he can see the graze. Gently he wipes away the dried blood, leaving behind a saffron-yellow stain. I wince at the sting. 'Used to do this for Jack when he was a tacker,' he mumbles as he works. 'Never seen so many skinned knees on a boy.'

I try to laugh, but the sting is washing tears into my eyes that won't blink away.

'Doesn't hurt that bad, does it?' Mel says, as they begin to spill over.

'No, it's not that.' I wipe my nose on my sleeve. 'It's . . . the cottage, Mel. The valley. I don't know what to do.'

He nods, screwing the lid back on the iodine. 'This is about Tremennor's claim on Enysyule, yes?' I must look shocked, because he chuckles drily. 'No secrets in Lanford. I heard it last night from old Derek, Liza's granddad.'

'Michaela seems about ready to give up,' I tell him, grateful that I don't have to explain the situation all over again. 'She and Liza were talking like it's a done deal already. Whatever scare tactic Roger's using on them, it's working.'

'Ah, well, they've got their business to think of,' Mel says, tracing a shape on the table. 'Being out of work's a serious thing in a place like this. If Michaela lost the agency, she'd have to move away. And I'll wager Tremennor's not making idle threats.'

'People treat him like he's still in charge,' I burst. 'Lord of the bloody manor. They don't have to obey him any more.'

Mel pushes back his chair. 'No, but the old ways run deep. For hundreds of years, "Tremennor" was as good as "master". Tough to break a habit of centuries.' He stands up, wanders over to the kitchen cupboards. "Specially when there's money involved. Not a lot of it, round here. Makes it powerful.' He comes back to the table, clutching a bottle and two glasses.

I try to recall Thomasina's graffitied newspaper article, feeling like I'm clutching at straws. 'I read that people were protesting the marina plans, that they don't even want one here. Can't we ask them to protest against him claiming Enysyule too?'

Mel shakes his head. 'That marina's a wrong-headed idea. Any child who can rig a sail will tell you it wouldn't work on this part of the Lan. They'd have to butcher the river. It'd spell the end for the yard, too.' He looks down at his hands. 'But I have to be honest with you, Jessie. Folk round here won't get involved in a fight for Enysyule. Not with a Tremennor. It's . . .' he sighs, 'a private matter, and an old one at that.'

'So what am I supposed to do?' I demand, feeling the tears rise again. 'Just sit and wait to be evicted?'

'Now, that's not what I said,' Roscarrow replies calmly. 'Listen, Roger's pedalling a bunch of lies if he says that valley belongs to him. Enysyule was Thomasina's, as much as it was anyone's. It was given to her mother, by one of the Tremennors.'

'*What?*' I lean forward, gripping the table. ' "Given" in what way? How do you know?'

He shrugs. 'Just do. Everyone does.'

I can't keep down a noise of frustration. 'Well, no one told me. Michaela said that Roger Tremennor has some kind of proof, something Thomasina signed, saying the land wasn't hers.'

Mel snorts dismissively. 'He can't have. Tremennors gave it back to her mother. They knew it wasn't theirs, however much they pretended it to be. They never even lived there, so far as I know.'

'So *why* did they give it back?' I press. 'They must have had a reason.'

Mel makes a baffled face. 'No idea. Maybe they produced a decent person for a change, by accident.'

I lean back and rub at my forehead. The smell of iodine fills my nose. 'Mel,' I say, 'this doesn't help. Roger says he has proof, so I need some too. That means deeds, documents, not hearsay and stories.'

He works the cork from the brandy bottle. 'Stories are all I have,' he says. 'And they're important, more important than papers and contracts. They're how we know the land, how we remember.'

'They're how you hold on to grudges,' I retort. 'I've seen it happen again and again, always the same, Tremennor and Roscarrow and Enysyule between you—' I stop, wondering if I've said too much.

Mel only looks at me steadily. 'You're not wrong,' he says in the end. 'That is how it's always been. Sometimes I'm even sorry for it.' He raises the bottle of brandy. 'But not today. Today the Tremennors can shave their heads and go east.'

He pours two generous measures of brandy, even though it's barely after twelve, and pushes one towards me.

'To steady your nerves,' he says.

'And what about your nerves?' I say, picking up the glass. 'Do they need steadying?'

'Most days.' He raises the glass to me. 'To Enysyule.'

Despite my reservations, Mel is right. The brandy warms my throat, washes the empty feeling from my belly. Just as I am about to swallow the last of it, I hear the front door slam, footsteps on the stairs.

'Been to see Mum,' Jack's voice calls, 'she sent me back with some ham.' He stops at the top of the stairs when he sees the pair of us sitting there, drinking our pre-afternoon brandies.

'Care to stay for lunch, Miss Pike?' Mel asks innocently.

Jack looks away when I try to meet his eyes. I can barely believe that this wary stranger is the same man I sat beside the fire with, toasting saffron buns. 'Thanks,' I say, 'but I'd better get back.'

Jack mutters something about making phone calls, and disappears upstairs.

'Don't let it get you down, Jessie,' says Mel, clapping me on the shoulder. 'We'll find a way to show up old Tremennor for the liar he is.'

I smile gratefully, follow him downstairs. Outside, Mel kicks at the signs I dragged out of the wood.

'Want these back?'

'God no.' I wrap my scarf around my neck. 'Burn them for all I care.'

'They'll make decent kindling,' Mel says, before scratching at his chin thoughtfully. 'Planning on going to town tonight, were you?'

Tonight . . . Of course. The Christmas light switch-on. With everything that's been happening I'd completely forgotten about it.

'I'm not sure,' I say hesitantly. 'It's been a long day already.'

'Go on,' he nudges. When I make a non-committal noise he smiles at me. 'To be honest I'm just angling for someone to walk me up there. Jack's got other plans, and my legs aren't as good as they once were.'

'All right,' I concede with a laugh. 'Where shall I meet you?'

'By the bridge.' He gathers up the signs. 'At six. And don't forget to wrap up warm!'

As I turn away, I see him scampering back up the stairs, almost, I think with a smile, as if there were nothing wrong with his legs in the slightest.

* * *

Across the land, winter advances, day by day gaining the upper hand. A foot slips, a head droops; fire flares in the darkness, a beacon, a brazen show of strength. The old year flees, headlong, towards it.

* * *

I hum a tune as I wait for Mel by the bridge. Whatever the song is, it's been going round and round my head all afternoon, like the lost end of a reel of cotton. I even hummed it to Perrin earlier as we played with a piece of string. He's been kittenish today, dashing about the house as though he had a fire at the end of his tail.

Up the hill, I can see the bright red eyes of cars, parking on the edge of the village, hear the squeal of children and the bustle of people filling the narrow streets. Despite my earlier protests, I'm glad I've come. Although – I check my phone – Mel is late. Perhaps he'll say his old legs were playing him up.

A chill wind surges up the riverbank, bringing the smell of the grey, winter sea. I narrow my eyes against it, imagining a boat with black-painted sides being tossed to and fro upon the dark waves, waiting for the tide to turn. It's too cold to stand in the wind for long, and just as I'm about to take the dark path down towards the creek to see where's Mel's got to, a torch flashes, and I see the edge of a green waxed jacket, hear the sound of footsteps.

'I was about to give up on you!' I call.

Jack Roscarrow emerges from the darkness, staring at me in astonishment. I draw back, embarrassed once again, and look over his shoulder.

'Is your grandfather—?'

'Is my grandfather—?'

Our eyes meet, and for a moment, I think he's going to burst out laughing, before he grimaces, turns off the torch.

'Mel asked me to meet him here,' I say hurriedly. 'At six. He said you had other plans.'

'He told me the same.'

'Oh.' For some reason, I don't know what to do with my hands. I tuck them into my jacket pockets. 'So . . . is he coming?'

'I doubt it. If I know him, he's already at the pub.' Finally, Jack looks me in the eye. 'I think this is his remarkably unsubtle way of saying he'd like us to be friends.'

'Ah.'

There's a long silence.

'Well,' Jack gestures to the village. 'You go on ahead, and I'll—'

'Don't be stupid,' I say, before wincing. 'I mean, you're going up there anyway, aren't you? We might as well walk together. Unless you don't want to be seen with me.' It's meant as a joke, but comes out sounding serious.

'Don't be stupid,' he says, with a glimmer of a smile.

In a vaguely effervescent silence, we make our way into the village. I've never seen so many people about, not even at Allantide. They crowd the streets, wrapped in scarves and hats, children swaddled in so many layers they can barely move. It's a chill, damp night, and the wind from the sea makes people shiver and grip their collars. Thankfully though, the rain is holding off. The sharpness of smoke catches in my nose, the warmth of roast chestnuts and sweet, mulled cider.

The café-post-office-bait-shop is still open, has put extra chairs outside, around a sort of brazier. I wave to Reg from the village shop as we pass.

'Do you want to grab a seat?' I ask Jack, before I change my mind. 'There's a couple free.'

'No,' he says, staring off towards the pub.

Indignation flares through me. He's not even trying to be friendly. 'Fine, well, have a good night,' I tell him, turning away.

'Wait!' He touches my shoulder. 'I didn't mean . . . I meant I didn't want to sit *here*. The best place to watch the lights is from the pub steps. Always has been.'

'Oh.' Is that an invitation? 'Well—'

'Look, I'll show you.'

We weave through the crowds pressed into Lanford's main street. There's a holiday feeling in the air; an innocent, child-ish one, as though the Yuletide is taking its first steps and we must cheer it on. On a makeshift stage near the pub, a group of teenagers are playing a reedy version of 'God Rest Ye Merry, Gentlemen' while small children dance about at the front.

I listen to the familiar carol in disbelief. Can it really be only a month until Christmas? It seems like yesterday that I took an impulsive train ride from London, chasing a dream here at the very end of summer.

'This way,' Jack calls, heading for a set of stone steps that lead up the side of the pub. They're already crowded with people, who budge up when they see Jack, shaking hands and slapping him on the shoulder. As always, they eye me curi-ously, but the mood is jovial and when I smile at them, they smile in return. Jack shifts so that I can wedge myself at the edge of the stairs, and when I look up, I see that he's right: from here, above the heads of the crowd, we can see the whole village, stretching towards the river.

I hear a familiar roar of laughter. Mel is sitting on a bench in front of the pub, pint in hand, surrounded by a posse of old men. His lined face breaks into a grin when he looks up and sees me watching. Beside me, Jack shakes a fist in mock-anger and Mel laughs uproariously, before going back to his drinking.

'He's an old devil,' Jack mutters. I sneak a look over at him, as he turns to talk to one of the other young men on the steps. Without his guard up he's open, friendly, even playful. I can't believe I got him so wrong.

'Look,' he leans down and I feel his warmth, radiating on my face. 'There's Dan and his tormenters!'

Sure enough, Liza's husband Dan is shepherding a brood of small children onto the stage with some difficulty. They stomp behind him, knocking into each other and jumping and fidgeting. One by one, he corrals them into a rough line. All of them have tinsel stuck to their coats and hats, and Dan himself is wearing a truly horrible jumper with flashing holly berries on it. He kneels at the edge of the stage and picks up a guitar.

'Here we go,' Jack says, grinning. 'The glamorous event itself. Aren't you glad you came?'

I laugh and turn back to watch. Someone introduces the children as Acorn Class of Lanford Primary School, who have the honour of switching on the lights this year. Dan strums a chord on his guitar. Picked up by the microphones, it echoes across the village.

'OK,' I hear him whisper, 'just like we practised. And go!'

All the children start singing different notes at once, but soon they fall into roughly the same rhythm. Beneath, I can hear Dan's clear voice, accompanying them.

'*Ha'n kelynn yw an kynsa a'n gwydh oll y'n koes* . . .'

Something shifts in my mind, like the tooth of a gear, clunking into place.

'I know this song,' I whisper. It's the one that's been chasing its tail around my head all day. How can I know it? I don't even understand the words. 'What is it?'

'It's Cornish,' Jack smiles fondly, 'an old carol. We all learn it at school when we're kids.' He waits as the children stumble through the rest of the verse before joining in: '*And the first tree in the greenwood, it was the holly.*'

'*Kelynn! Kelynn!*'

A man walking through a snowstorm, singing to keep himself warm, to keep the fear from his heart . . .

'*Holly! Holly!*'

The last chords of the song merge with the clapping of the crowd. There's a flurry of activity on the stage, and all at once, the town bursts into life. Lights shoot into the darkness, white, gold, red, even blue, every colour a flame could be. The crowd *ooh* and *aah* but the noise is fading in my ears, replaced by a dull roaring, and it's not electric lights I'm seeing – it's torches, held aloft in many hands, driving away the darkness. Voices are raised around a grey stone, and through it all I hear feet running, hooves hammering, a heart thundering, a woman singing, a knife chiselling stone, tears falling on snow . . .

My head spins. I put out a hand to steady myself, and grip nothing but air. For one horrible second I think I will fall; then a hand grabs my coat, pulls me back. I'm on the steps, the crowd still *ooh*ing before me, hundreds of colourful lights illuminating the streets of Lanford.

Jack is peering into my face. ' . . . all right?' he's asking.

I swallow the roar from my ears and nod, shifting away from the side of the steps. He doesn't look convinced.

'Do you want a drink?' he shouts, over the announcements that are taking place on stage. 'Now's a good time, there's no queue!'

I nod again, keen to get off the stairs, away from the carpet of lights that are now shining so innocently in my blurred vision. With relief, I step down onto the ground. Outside the pub, there's a stand selling mulled cider. I insist on paying for them; the coins give me something concrete to focus on, something normal. As Jack buys some roast chestnuts, I take a sip. Spices wrap around me, achingly familiar; cinnamon, cloves, dried peel, mingled with the sharpness of apples that a few months ago were hanging heavy in an orchard.

By some unspoken agreement, we begin to wander away from the crowd, taking a tiny backstreet down towards the water. It's quieter here, the sounds of revelry fading behind us. I breathe in deeply. Perhaps I'm growing too accustomed to the quiet of the valley.

'What happened, back there?' Jack asks, sipping at his cider. 'You looked like you were about to pass out.'

I fill my mouth with hot cider, buying time to think.

'I don't know,' I say after a minute. 'My imagination has a habit of running away with me lately.' I summon up a smile. 'I think it's the Enysyule effect. Was Thomasina . . . did she ever see things?'

Jack makes a noise. 'Not sure. Wouldn't rule it out though, she certainly was strange.' He looks sidelong at me. 'She used to talk to Perrin like he wasn't a cat at all, more of a companion she shared the valley with.'

I don't say anything, glad for the darkness that hides my face. We reach the bottom of the hill, where the road meets the river. Jack sits, lets his feet dangle over the edge. I follow suit. In front of us, the dark water reflects the town's illuminations, gold and red and green.

'Thank you for bringing that sketchbook round the other day,' he says after a while. 'Grandpa's been showing it to me. It really does mean a lot to him.'

'It was nothing,' I murmur, warming my hands on the paper cup.

'No, it wasn't.' Jack looks over. 'Listen, I'm sorry if I've been—' He stops, shaking his head, as though he can't find the words he wants. 'Were you OK earlier?' he asks instead. 'I saw that the iodine was out.'

I laugh, pull up my sleeve to show the big, yellow stain on my arm. 'It was just a scratch. I didn't even know people still used iodine.'

'They don't. I think Grandpa's had that bottle since about 1964.'

'He said you were pretty familiar with it.'

Jack takes the chestnuts out of his pocket, offers them to me. 'I was what you'd call an "accident prone" child. Used to treat the yard like a playground, winches and cables and broken motors and all.'

'When did you start working there?' Steam rises from the nut as I shell it, releasing the sweet, charred flavour.

'I've always helped out. I was away to uni for a while. Then Grandma Phyllis died and Grandpa couldn't cope on his own so,' he shrugs, 'I graduated early and came back. Been working with him ever since.'

'What about the rest of your family?'

'What about them?' he asks. 'You mean why don't they work there?' I nod. 'They've got jobs of their own. Mum's a book-keeper, Dad runs a garage, inland. He's never been into boats. And my sister Amy couldn't care less about what's on top of the water, only what's underneath it. She's a marine biologist, works abroad.' He inspects another nut. 'So that leaves me.'

I can't help but picture the big Roscarrow family at Enysyule, celebrating before the hearth. Three brothers and a father, all hanged. Even generations later, the effect still lingers. For the first time, I begin to understand why the grudge between the Tremennors and the Roscarrows runs so strong.

'Jack,' I ask, 'do you know how Thomasina and her mother came to be at Enysyule? All Mel could tell me were stories. I need to know for certain.'

He looks across. 'Because of Roger? Grandpa told me what he's up to.' He fidgets with his empty cup. 'I'm guessing Alex is in on it as well?'

Despite the cold, I feel my cheeks start to burn. I was hoping he wouldn't bring Alex up, but, as I'm starting to understand, Jack Roscarrow is nothing if not forthright.

'He must have known about it the whole time,' I say quietly.

Jack makes a face. 'I'm sorry.'

'Don't *you* apologise. Honestly, I don't know what he was thinking.' I pause. 'I don't know what *I* was thinking.'

Jack keeps his mouth firmly shut.

'If you say "I told you so", I'll—'

'Wouldn't dream of it,' he replies, flashing a grin, just like Mel's. 'To answer your question, no, I don't know any more than Grandpa. It's the nature of this place. Stories are our history, and our history is built on stories. Rarely facts. I'm sorry I can't tell you more.' All at once, his face lights up. 'But you should go and see Geoff, Michaela's husband. He runs the local museum, knows the actual history of this place better than anyone. He's an outsider,' he nudges me, 'like you. He isn't caught up in all the local legends.'

'Surely Michaela will have asked him already?'

Jack shrugs. 'Maybe. But there's a chance she hasn't asked the right questions.'

'And I will?'

Jack smiles and I find myself taking in his every feature; his tanned face, his strong nose, his eyes, bright as the hazel wood, shifting constantly between solemnity and mirth.

'Yes, you will,' he says softly.

We look at each other for a moment longer. I can feel the heat of his body near mine, catch his scent, woodsmoke and soap and warm skin.

'Well,' I look away over the river, trying to hide the flush upon my cheeks. 'In that case I'll go and see Geoff tomorrow. Where did you say the museum was?'

'Next to the church.' Jack sits back, and the cold, November air rushes to fill the space between us. 'Though it won't be open tomorrow. In fact, I'm pretty sure it's only open Tuesdays and Thursdays.'

I groan. 'The meeting with Tremennor is on Monday. I was hoping to have some answers by then.'

'Tell you what,' Jack says, jumping to his feet, 'let's go and ask Grandpa's friends. They'll be well pickled by now. Even if they don't remember anything useful, they'll be good fun.'

Instinctively I hold out a hand and he pulls me up, until we're standing close.

'Your grandpa's friends,' I ask hurriedly, starting to walk, 'they're not the same ones from that time in the pub, when I . . .?'

'When you marched over and gave us all a good talking to?' Jack laughs. 'Yep. That's them.'

'Oh god.'

'Don't worry, Miss Pike.' We emerge onto the main street, its strings of Christmas lights gaudy in the darkness. Outside the pub, Mel spots us and bellows. Jack grins in response. 'You've met the worst of them already.'

It's with a queasy stomach that I get dressed on Monday morning, trying to find my smartest, most serious clothes to wear for the meeting with Tremennor and his lawyer. Normally I'd be writing at this time of day, sitting at the kitchen table, wrapped in a huge, old cardigan, drinking my third cup of tea. Perrin has his own routine. As soon as I sit down to work, the pantry window squeaks and paws scamper into the main room, carrying a wet and muddy cat, intent on walking all over my keyboard. That done, he takes himself off to the old armchair by the fire, has his morning bath, and goes to sleep.

Today, he doesn't look very pleased when he sees me standing by the door, rather than sitting in my usual place. He leaps up onto the table anyway, leaving prints all over the wood. I stroke him carefully, trying not to get cat hair all over my clothes.

'Wish me luck,' I tell him. 'I'm going to fight for your home.'

He chirrups and heads off towards the fire. I wish I could do the same. As it is, all I can do is potter around, getting steadily more nervous. Just as it's coming up to the hour, I hear the bleep of a message. It must be Liza, saying she's at the top of the lane. The phone is on the edge of the dresser, in the one spot that sometimes picks up a signal. The noise has piqued Perrin's interest; he jumps up onto the dresser to sniff the phone curiously. Strange, I think as I head over, he's never shown any interest in the past.

'Perrin,' I say warningly as he prods at it.

He stops, one paw raised, surveying me with those knowing yellow eyes. Then, almost thoughtfully, he lowers his paw and shoves the phone from the edge of the dresser.

'Perrin!' I lunge for it, too late. It hits the flagstones with a crack and skitters away into a dark corner.

Of course, he takes no notice of my aggravation, just begins to wash the guilty paw as if the phone has somehow soiled it. Swearing, I get down on my knees to peer under the dresser. It's a horror-scape of neglect; cobwebs and thick clumps of dust, grit of unknown origin, woodlice, spiders, and now, in the far corner, my phone. *So much for looking tidy and smart,* I think, as I lay flat on my stomach in order to retrieve it, wincing as webs break against my outstretched fingers. Even then, it's too far to reach, and I have to use the poker to drag it towards me.

As I do, it catches on something heavy, and I hear the scrape of broken glass. Not my phone, *that* emerges dirty but unscathed and flashing with messages. Liza is probably waiting for me … Hurriedly I clatter around with the poker again, until I manage to nudge whatever it is into my reach. My fingers touch something that feels like wood, and I pull the thing free.

It's a frame, long darkened by time and smoke, the glass broken into three pieces. A black velvet backing holds two round discs of bronze. *Medals?* I wonder. A broken string trails from the back. It must have snapped at some point, fallen behind the dresser, unnoticed. My fingers hover over the grimy glass. It's as if the discs are magnetic, are pulling me in, begging me to touch them …

My phone buzzes angrily on the floor, breaking my reverie. I snatch my hand away. No time now. Whatever the discs are, they'll have to wait until later. I shut them in a dresser drawer, just in case Perrin decides to be playful again. Then I'm grabbing my bag, my coat, dropping the crumb-covered phone into my pocket. As I close the door, I glance over at Perrin, ensconced in his chair by the fire. He blinks at me. If I didn't know better, I'd say he looked smug.

'Where've you been?' Liza asks, as I climb into the car, sweaty from power-walking up to the lane, dusty from retrieving my phone. 'We don't want to be late for this thing, seriously.'

'Sorry. Perrin . . . Never mind. Hi, Michaela.'

Michaela nods from the back seat without looking up. Scattered all around her are papers and files and notebooks. She's wearing a smart suit of eye-watering red, her hair sprayed so firmly into place it looks like a helmet.

'She's checking for loopholes,' Liza murmurs to me, as we speed away, 'anything to prove we have a superior position to Roger.'

'I asked Mel Roscarrow about it over the weekend,' I tell her, 'and his friends. They were pretty much unanimous that Enysyule was given to Thomasina's mother, about a hundred years ago, but none of them could remember how or why.'

'Then it's no use to us, I'm afraid,' says Liza, grim-faced.

'What about . . . deeds for the land, or something?' I persist. 'Surely someone must know.'

'The deeds are missing,' says a gloomy voice from the back seat. I look around into Michaela's slightly reddened eyes. 'It's why Roger thinks he has a chance; he's going to apply for a new set, submitting proof that the land is his.'

I slump back in frustration, and stay there until we turn off the road. RIVERVIEW GOLF CLUB, a sign announces, MEMBERS ONLY. No one says anything as we're funnelled along a curving driveway. All around, the scratchy brown hedgerows and yellow-flecked gorse bushes have been replaced by neat grass, clipped to the nearest millimetre.

We make a bizarre troupe, walking into the foyer of the golf club, me in a crumpled, dusty blazer, Michaela in garish, shoulder-padded red, Liza prim and ponytailed, a bundle of files under her arm. For one thing, it seems like we're the only women for miles.

'This way,' the young man on reception says, looking fearfully over his shoulder at us. 'Mr Tremennor has booked the Garden Suite. He's here already.'

'Of course he is,' Michaela says sourly, as we follow the boy down a thickly carpeted hallway, the walls hung with photographs of past members.

Through a pair of smoked-glass doors, I see Roger Tremennor, leaning casually on a meeting table, an empty coffee cup before him. Opposite is a younger man in a slim-fitting suit, who laughs, tapping something out on his phone. I swallow drily, feeling like I've slipped into another world, one of legally binding language and airless conference suites, a thousand miles from the wild, secluded greenness of Enysyule, where the only reality is stone and root and water.

Roger Tremennor makes a show of standing up and extending his hand, only for Michaela to brush straight past him. I supress a bleak smile. She may not be holding out much hope for Enysyule, but she certainly isn't going to be gracious about it. She hauls out the chair at the head of the table and drops into it.

'All right,' she says, 'let's get on with it. You're Mr Mitchell, are you,' she directs at the younger man, 'the solicitor from Truro?' When the man opens his mouth to answer, she ignores him, ploughs on. 'This is Ms Graff, my assistant, and Miss Pike, who is renting Enysyule.'

'A pleasure to meet you all,' the man says smoothly, 'though I did say in my letter that it wasn't necessary for the tenant to be present.'

The tenant. My jaw clenches. 'If my lease is going to be invalidated I want to know why,' I tell him.

He only smiles pleasantly, as though I've said nothing of consequence. 'So,' he says, 'shall we start by going over the current situation?'

'We know what the current situation is, thank you,' Michaela snaps. 'What we don't know is what Roger here is playing at.'

'Now, Michaela, I'm not the one who went back on her word.' Tremennor leans over the table, his hands folded. 'We as good as agreed that I would take on Enysyule.'

'No, we did not. We talked about it in *theory* before I advertised the cottage, which, I'll remind you, was a condition of the trust fund. It's not my fault Miss Pike signed on the line before you.'

'This is the fund,' interrupts Mr Mitchell, peering at his phone screen, 'that was set up to "provide a guardian and protector for Enysyule for as long as Perrin shall live"?'

'Yes,' Michaela says coldly.

'And Perrin is . . .?'

I watch a muscle in her cheek twitch. 'A cat.'

'A cat,' Mr Mitchell repeats, staring her down. 'How unusual.'

'Unusual but entirely legal,' Liza says, tapping the folder before her. 'I have a copy of the paperwork here if you care to inspect it.'

I shoot her a small smile. The corners of her mouth lift in return.

'It's only legal if she actually owned the damn place,' Roger says loudly. 'Which she didn't. Enysyule is still, legally speaking, part of the Tremennor Estate.'

'That is *rubbish*!' Michaela's face as red as her suit. She takes a breath, trying to steady her voice. 'It was given to Thomasina's mother by one of your relatives and that's the truth. I know it, you know it, the whole village knows it.'

'The usual superstitious clap-trap,' sneers Tremennor.

'Now look here!' Michaela is half out of her chair, Roger rising to meet her.

'Really, there is no need for raised voices,' says Mr Mitchell. 'Mrs Welwyn, this matter could be resolved in a few minutes. All you need to do is produce some evidence. One piece. Can you do that?'

Michaela glares at him, gives a curt shake of her head.

'Well, seeing as Mr Tremennor has a signed statement from Miss Roscarrow acknowledging her status as a tenant, and given the dubious, ah, *feline* nature of the trust fund,' he smiles at us, 'I'm afraid you don't have a leg to stand on.'

He clicks a pen, and pulls a piece of paper towards him. 'So, let's talk settlement, shall we? Mr Tremennor is prepared to offer a generous sum for your cooperation.' He scrawls out a figure. 'This is our current offer.' He pushes the paper over to Michaela. I watch the colour in her cheeks curdle from red to white, and know that I can't hold my tongue any longer.

'This is bullshit,' my voice rings through the silence. 'What about Perrin? Thomasina wanted him to be cared for, *in the cottage*, for the rest of his life. It's why she set up the fund. Doesn't that count for anything?'

'As I understand it,' Mitchell says innocently, 'the animal is already very old. As soon as it dies, any prior agreement will be invalid. And then we'll have to go through all of this again. Which wouldn't be very sensible, would it?' He gives me a smile. 'After all, how long do cats really live?'

'"How long do cats really live",' I mutter, as we troop across the car park. 'What did he mean by that?' Around us, the day has turned even darker, the sky flat and headache-grey.

Nobody responds as we climb into the car. Liza starts the engine. Their silence is unnerving.

'So, what are we going to do?' I ask, turning around to include Michaela. 'If he's lying, there must be some way we can—' I stop. Michaela is bent over in the seat, her head in her hands.

'We can't do anything,' she says, voice muffled by her scarf. 'You saw how much money he's offering as a settle-ment. If he's willing to throw that much at keeping us quiet, he'll throw even more at making certain we're utterly crushed if this goes to court.' She looks up at me, face sagging. 'The business just can't afford that. I'm so sorry, Jess. If I'd known, I never would have let you sign that rental agreement.'

I turn away to stare out the window, barely holding back tears. The thought that Enysyule – the place where I feel most alive, most connected to something greater than myself – could be snatched away and destroyed forever is incompre-hensible, brings a pain in my chest that won't be rubbed away. And Perrin, abandoned once again, his home torn down . . . No. I close my eyes, trying to see some way forwards.

Enysyule, the name lingers in my thoughts, the way it has always done. *Grey and green. Saffron and rain. Torches in the darkness. Light on old stone. Holly trees and falling snow and a creature that moves on paws of smoke, claws like brambles and eyes the colour of the harvest moon . . .*

'When do you need to give them an answer, about the settlement?' I ask abruptly.

'We've got five working days to respond,' Michaela says, frowning at me. 'So next Monday.'

'Give me until then.' I look at them both. 'Please, give me a few days to try and find a way out of this. You owe me that much, at least.'

Michaela sighs. 'All right,' she says. 'We hold off until Monday. But please don't get your hopes up, Jess. Around here, a Tremennor is a hard thing to fight.'

The church is on the outskirts of the village. Along the light-strung main street, past the pub, and after the last of the thatched cottages, is a path that leads to the top of the hill. The church stands there, solitary, overlooking Lanford to one side, the river and its hidden creeks to the other. I stop on the road before it, catching my breath. It's a strange building, the architecture somewhat ragged, as though it has been added to and repaired by many hands over the centuries. A squat, grey tower rises from one end, the stone battered by the winds.

St. Piran's Church, reads a faded wooden sign beside the entrance. A gate with a pitched roof opens onto a grassy grave-yard. It's a lychgate, I realise, as I step through, a gate of the dead, and a very old one at that. The churchyard is old too, gravestones jutting from the ground at crazy angles. Carved letters catch my eye, and I wander closer to see familiar names repeated again and again. Roscarrows and Graffs, Blyths and Heskeths and Polkinghornes, but, I notice, no Tremennors. They probably have their own, private plot. I make my way towards the very edge of the graveyard, where a group of wind-twisted trees stand before a steep drop, down towards the riverbank. Here, there are no fresh flowers, or faded candles. The grass is longer, the stones deeply weathered. Many have fallen or cracked, and lie in pieces, being slowly swallowed by the ground. I bend down, trying to decipher some of the lichen-covered letters, and the wind picks up, buffeting its way through the claw-like trees, slapping my cheeks with cold. Above, sea birds scream on the wind.

'Can I help you?' asks someone by my elbow, and I nearly jump out of my skin.

It's Geoff, Michaela's husband. He's holding a thick ring binder, peering at me through round glasses. 'Oh, Miss Pike,' he says, eking out a smile. 'Hello. I heard you might be stopping by.'

I still forget how small Lanford is at times. 'Hello. Er – yes.' We stare at each other. 'So, are you open?'

'Of course,' Geoff rushes, 'of course, I'd just nipped out for some lunch. Come with me.'

Tacked onto the back of the church is a single-storey, barn-type building that I assume must once have been a church hall. A plastic plaque beside the heavy wooden door reads LANFORD VILLAGE MUSEUM. Inside, it's dark and chilly, and as Geoff flicks on the lights, I see that the entire place is jammed floor-to-ceiling with history. Well-used display cases line the walls, containing huge, leather-bound books, coins, farm equipment, fragments of pottery, flints and arrowheads. The walls are thick with framed displays of old photographs and sketches, maps and newspaper clippings. The whole of Lanford's history, thousands of years of births and deaths and marriages, hundreds of harvests and yields and Yuletides, are abridged in this room.

I stare at it all in astonishment. In comparison to this, my own life seems brief, feverish, and for the first time I understand the sense of heaviness I always feel when stepping across the boundary of Enysyule; it's the weight of time, centuries collecting in a single valley, like rain in a hollow.

'Sorry about the mess in here,' mumbles Geoff, breaking through my thoughts. 'We need a bigger place, really.' He smiles apologetically, turning on a couple of electric heaters to warm the chilly space.

'This is . . . incredible,' I tell him, staring at a collection of tin objects. 'Do you run it all by yourself?'

'Well, we have a few volunteers from time to time,' he says, looking around the place critically, 'but yes, I find myself doing the bulk of the work. It's not always so quiet as this, it can get quite busy in the summer.'

I smile back at this calm, self-contained man, wondering how on earth he and the whirlwind that is Michaela ended up together.

'I'm guessing you already know why I'm here?' I ask, shifting closer to one of the heaters.

'Yes,' he sighs, 'it's a sorry business. I've never seen Michaela so anxious, and it takes a lot to ruffle her.' He disappears off into an alcove. I follow to find a cupboard masquerading as an office, an old computer and a chair barely visible among mountains of archive boxes, crates and files. I watch as Geoff deposits the ring binder onto a towering stack, and slides carefully onto the chair. 'I'm terribly afraid I'm not going to be very helpful,' he says, turning on the machine. 'I've already had a good think on it myself, done a bit of digging.'

'I talked to Mel Roscarrow,' I tell him, leaning in the doorway, 'he said that Enysyule was given back to Thomasina's mother by one of the Tremennors. He didn't know any details though.'

'The same story I've had, from everyone in town,' Geoff agrees, 'hardly useful is it? But I used it to work out some vague dates.' He squints around, and finally locates a stool, underneath a stack of folders. 'Here, take those off and have a seat.'

His manner has changed completely from the reserved, almost aloof man I met in the pub. He's eager and lively here, surrounded by dusty boxes and fragments of the past. I wedge myself onto the stool, and he opens a spreadsheet, filled with what looks like some kind of truncated family tree.

'I checked the census records,' he tells me, scrolling through. 'The change of ownership – if that's what it was

– must have taken place some time after 1911.' He points. 'There's Thomasina's mother, Violet. According to the 1911 census she and her husband and son are living with the rest of the Roscarrows, by the river.'

'What about the next census?' I ask, leaning in. 'Are they at Enysyule then?'

Geoff smiles patiently. 'No way of knowing,' he says. 'That census hasn't been released yet.'

I sit back in frustration. 'What about maps, or village records?' I ask. 'There *must* be something that keeps track of who owns what around here.'

'Maps don't usually mention ownership. But I thought the very same thing. So I had a quick look through the District Valuation Records, you know?'

I have no idea what he's talking about, nod along anyway, caught up in his enthusiasm.

'They show ownership for the whole district, from 1909 to 1915.' He clicks busily at the mouse, and slowly an image resolves itself on the screen, a scanned page of a book. He beams over at me. 'I stopped by the records office in town the other day and asked them to copy the page on Enysyule for me.' His smile wavers. 'I'm afraid it's not what you want to hear.'

'It was still owned by the Tremennors in 1915?'

'Indeed. And I can't find any other references after that.' He huffs. 'All a bit vexing. Of course, if we had access to the Tremennor Estate Records . . .' He raises his eyebrows at me meaningfully. 'Though I'm guessing there's a reason Roger Tremennor hasn't produced those as evidence.'

'Couldn't a court force him to hand them over?' I ask, trying not to sound impatient.

'Not really. They're private records, you see, no one knows what's there. Roger could just' – he mimes whisking something away – 'and say the relevant record has been lost or never existed at all.' He leans back in his creaky chair. 'I'm sorry Miss Pike. It's a bit of a catch-22.'

I gaze into space, watching the flickering lines of the elderly computer monitor. 'So there's nothing else?' I say flatly. 'No records I can search?'

'I had wondered about trying the council minutes from the nineteen tens and twenties,' Geoff says, 'to see if there's any mention of Enysyule. But they're not digitised. It'd be like searching for a needle in a haystack.'

'I could look though?' I sit up on the stool so quickly I almost cause an avalanche of papers. 'I could see them, just in case?'

'Yes,' says Geoff doubtfully. 'I suppose. I do have them in storage here. I'd have to remember where I put them . . .'

After a few minutes of gentle persuasion, and one offer of volunteering help, Geoff shows me down into the basement of the hall. It's freezing down here, stone walls and a stone floor that reminds me a little too much of a crypt. The electric lights are garish overhead and don't do much to illuminate the corners. Just like the room above, it is packed with items, bookshelves sagging under ledgers and boxes, plastic crates stacked one atop the other, large objects lurking in the shadows, covered in dust sheets. Geoff picks his way through it all with experienced ease.

'Here we are,' he mutters, peering up at a bookcase of threadbare spines, 'the Parish Council – no, those are the Treasurer's books.' He stretches on his toes. 'Ah! Yes, this is what we want.' He heaves down a squat, leather-bound book as thick as a bible and places it in my arms.

LANFORD PARISH MINUTE BOOK, it says in faded ink on the front, 1887–1916.

'And you'll want these too, I think.' Geoff follows it up with a second one, and a third. 'That should take you up to about 1940.'

There's no space to sit at the desk, so Geoff lets me camp out on the floor near one of the heaters so I can go through the books. I open the first one, marvelling at the neat, cursive handwriting that fills the page.

This meeting of the parish council was held on 15th January 1887, at 7 o'clock in the evening. There were 12 parishioners present.

I turn the page. The same format, only three months later, again and again, pages of it. I shift on the scratchy carpet, trying to get comfortable. I'm going to be here for a while. I flick through, the old spine creaking, until I reach 1915, when Enysyule was still in the hands of the Tremennors. *Please*, I beg it silently, settling the book in my lap, *tell me something*.

The minutes offer a glimpse into the daily life of Lanford over a hundred years ago. I turn the pages, marked by dozens of pairs of hands. There are disputes over who must cut a hedge, who has mooring rights, and whether the postman could be persuaded to carry out an evening collection. As the year runs out and becomes another, it's clear that even Lanford did not escape the horrors that were shaking the rest of the world.

1916 is almost entirely blank; a few hurried notes for one curt annual meeting. In 1917 the minutes start up again, though not for a positive reason. The shadows of war spread across the pages like spilled ink. There's a plea to the Tremennor Estate to turn woodland into allotments, refused by the steward, since his master is away on commission in France. There are food shortages, coal shortages, people burning fence posts to stay warm . . . Until finally, in the last meeting of 1918, there's mention of the armistice.

And yet, still nothing concerning Enysyule. Through the museum's tiny window, I see the daylight starting to fade. Geoff brings me over a cup of tea and a biscuit – with due warning not to spill anything – and tells me he has to close in an hour. I turn back to the book, trying to ignore the gnawing of disappointment in my stomach.

1919 is filled with war memorials and Peace Day celebrations, but also death duties, high taxation. In the back room, I hear Geoff turning off the computer, getting ready to leave. Feverishly, I scan through the pages. August, October, December . . . I'm about to flick on to the next year, a new decade, when a word catches my eye, the curve of an 'e', the downward swoops of two 'y's. I grip the edges of the book.

Letter from Colonel Tremennor regarding situation at Enysyule. Duly noted by Parish Council.

The next line moves on to the state of the village drains. I stare at it, dumbstruck, searching back through the text before and after for any other mention. *What situation?* I want to yell at it. *What do you mean?* It's no use; whoever wrote that neat sentence is long gone, has taken the knowledge with them.

Geoff tuts when I show him the entry. 'Lazy note takers,' he says, 'are the bane of a historian's existence.' He pats me on the arm. 'You're most welcome to come back another day and keep looking, if you want.'

I shake my head, unable to speak. Something tells me that the 'situation' in 1919 is exactly the moment in Enysyule's history I've been searching for, and yet, as proof, it's useless. Nevertheless, I take a quick picture of the page on my phone, before Geoff returns the books to the basement.

Outside the church, a breeze is swirling up from the river, wrapping chill arms around me, as it must have done to so many people in the dark days of 1918. Slowly, empty-handedly, I make my way downhill towards Enysyule, the strings of Christmas lights flickering on behind me.

★　　★　　★

The land does not live as humans live. It endures, as they do not. It ages, yet is renewed, like a rock pool, filled and worn by the sea.

But still, it can reflect their presence; it can changed forever by their choices, fair or foul ...

★ ★ ★

The evening passes quietly. I don't have any appetite, and only pick at dinner. Even I'm finally getting sick of beans on toast. Perrin seems to have caught some of my gloom, because he doesn't move from his chair, even when I put a dish of tinned mackerel down for him. It's not like him at all.

He barely raises his head when I kneel on the flagstones before the armchair, only blinks up at me listlessly. I stroke his head and whiskers. His nose is dry, I notice with concern, and he's floppy when I pick him up. He purrs on my lap, though not with his usual energy.

'Are you not well, little one?' I murmur, staring down at his half-closed eyes. A pang shoots through my chest, a pain that's almost physical when I consider the possibility that he might be ill, that something might happen to him. I can't even begin to image life here without him. He *is* Enysyule; he is the valley's soul, its beating heart. I put down fresh dishes of water for him, and when I go upstairs to bed, I carry him with me. He doesn't object, only curls into a ball on the blankets.

I hunch the covers around me against the cold. My body feels bone-weary, but my mind is another matter; a skittering mess of thoughts. I promised Perrin that I would keep his home safe, and yet, I don't know what else I can do to fight. Making a stand against Tremennor is like trying to stem a flood with my bare hands. I lie awake thinking, listening to the wind as it whispers down the chimney, to an owl, hooting in the darkness. I wish Perrin would arch his back and go to join it, singing all night to the moon.

Hours pass, somewhere between sleep and wakefulness, and still, Perrin doesn't stir. I've never known him so quiet. Finally, in the early hours of the morning, I find myself sitting up, laying a hand upon his side, to check that it rises and falls. One eye opens to look at me. In the scant glow from the fireplace, it glints like bronze. I feel my own eyes widen, and then I'm slipping out of the covers. The stairs are cold on my bare feet, the flagstones colder. How could I have forgotten?

The medals are exactly where I left them, resting quietly in the dresser drawer. I lift them out, the velvet backing soft against my fingers, almost like a living thing. I stir up the fire, for light and warmth, and hold them up to its red glow. They reflect the flames back, like two bronze eyes. There's a design upon their tarnished surfaces, and words . . . I frown and look closer.

'He died for freedom and honour,' I read, my voice a hushed whisper. A shiver runs through me as I realise; these aren't medals at all. They're memorial plaques. Fingertips trembling, I trace the names engraved upon each, a letter at a time.

Frank John Roscarrow. Thomas Peter Roscarrow.

Then, reflected in the bronze I see a flicker of movement, a quick shadow, slinking past.

'Perrin?' I call. The room behind me is empty. I look back to the fireplace, to the plaques, only to see movement in them once more. This time I don't turn; instead, I watch the reflection. After a moment, something moves. It's the front door, drifting open, inch by inch.

Once I would have hidden my head in fright. Now I stay perfectly still, although the breath dries up in my lungs. Finally I hear a distant woman's voice, a murmur of song, and turn around, just in time to see the end of a black tail whisk through the door.

'Wait—' I gasp, staggering to my feet. 'Perrin, wait!'

Outside it's dark still, pre-dawn. Far down the path I can see a flicker of light, like a lantern. I take one step forward, another.

'Wait . . .'

The next thing I know, I'm faced with a wall of thick, green leaves. I'm panting, I realise, though I don't remember running, don't even remember walking here. I bend over my knees to catch my breath. Above, the sky has changed colour. Not deep night any more but the colour of winter dusk, lilac and grey, delicate as chiffon.

I'm not alone. There's a woman sitting against the Perranstone, a baby cradled in her arms. I start to ask why she is here, but then I realise, I already know. She has come to fulfil the old promise, the one that ran in her husband's blood, and her son's; a promise that will now be her daughter's to keep. When the holly berries flush red, she knows, they must visit the valley. They must bring food, the best they can find. The fishermen were understanding when she told them where she was going, loaded her basket with what they could spare.

The dusk deepens. She will have to find her way home using the barn lantern. She shivers slightly, and the baby stirs, a tiny frown creasing her brow. The woman jogs her and begins to breathe a song, to soothe her back to sleep.

'*Ha'n kelynn yw an kynsa a'n gwydh oll y'n koes . . .*'

A flash of yellow, a rustle of leaves and the trees give up a black cat. It trots into the centre of the clearing, meows merging with the soft notes of the woman's song.

'*Hou*, Perrin,' she says, laying the baby in her lap.

The cat looks older than she remembers, black fur flecked with white. Still, he swaggers boldly to where she sits and sniffs at her boots, before going to rub himself against the stone, as though greeting an old friend. Next, he comes to inspect the baby in her lap, smelling it curiously. The woman keeps one eye on him as she unpacks her basket; he is, after all, a wild thing. But soon he draws away, satisfied. The baby has woken up, perhaps at the touch of the cat's wet nose.

She stares around drowsily, her blue eyes already flecked hazel.

'Very well, very well,' the woman murmurs to the cat, who is pawing at one of the newspaper-wrapped packets on the ground. She folds it open, revealing a gleaming fresh fish for the cat to fall upon. With a smile, she loosens the paper of two more packets and places them near the stone. At first she was worried other animals would come and take the food, but, the old fishermen assured her, every fox or badger or bird within miles knows better than to take food left for Perrin.

The cat purrs as he eats, pleased with his dinner of fresh fish, the sound filling the clearing. The baby is beginning to frown and fret, so the woman releases the buttons of her blouse. The winter air rushes to sting her warm skin. Hurriedly she wraps the shawl around her shoulders, brings the baby to her breast.

'*Kelynn . . . kelynn . . .*' she sings softly, staring down at the tiny child, her hope, her only reason to continue when everything was trampled and torn. A final gift from her husband, perfect and vital.

For a time, everything is peaceful; the sky deepening, the woman's breath misting in the soon-to-be frosty air. Soon she will have to return to the boatyard on the river, busy with cooking, crowded with family-in-law, determined to make this first Christmas of peacetime a merry one. But in this quiet hour she can be with her own family again, even if it is now just a family of two. *Or three, including himself*, she thinks with a smile.

She is about to ease the baby away, about to stand and light the lantern when the cat makes a noise. He is staring fixedly across the clearing. Through the dark trees, she sees a flicker of movement. Her eyes search desperately, thinking for one senseless moment that they have returned to her on this dark, Yuletide night, when the walls between the worlds are thin.

'Frank?' she calls, voice cracking. 'Tom?'

A man steps into the clearing. Of course, he is not either of them. He wears a military uniform beneath a greatcoat, ceremonial with ribbons and bright medals. His eyes meet hers, before travelling to the baby at her breast. He averts his gaze.

'I am sorry,' he says stiffly. 'I did not mean . . . I am looking for a Mrs Violet Roscarrow.'

'That's me,' the woman answers, re-arranging her blouse, pulling a handkerchief from her pocket to wind the baby. The man does not speak again. 'You were told I was here, I suppose?' she asks.

'Yes,' he says distantly. He is taking deep breaths, one hand on his chest, as if it hurts. His eyes light upon the cat, who has finished his meal and now sits, returning the man's stare.

'Uncommon strange,' the man mutters, before standing alert. 'Mrs Roscarrow,' he announces with grim resolution. 'I come with deepest condolences for your loss. Your husband and son fought valiantly for their country.' He reaches into the pocket of his greatcoat. 'Please accept these tokens of the Crown's grati- tude this Christmas, in recognition of their service.'

He thrusts a brown-paper-wrapped parcel out before him, like a soldier awaiting a command. For a long while, the woman does not answer, only strokes the baby's back. Living flesh, not cold, bitter metal. She holds her all the tighter.

'Whatever they are, I've no hands to take them,' she says quietly, 'if you'd be so kind as to put them in the basket there.'

The man frowns, his jaw clenching, and strides forward to place the parcel in the bottom of the basket. After that, he does not seem to know what to do, only stands, staring furi- ously at the ground.

'Mind unwrapping that bundle for me?' the woman asks, when it becomes clear he has no intention of moving. 'That one wrapped in newspaper, to my left?'

The man blinks, as though she has said something extraordinary, before nodding once.

'What is it?' he asks, face wrinkling at the slimy offerings within.

'Fish scraps. They're for him.' She nods over to the cat, still watching them closely. 'Take them over would you?'

'I'll not wait upon a cat,' the man retorts, colour returning to his face.

The woman says nothing, only rocks the baby as she grumbles. The man stares down at the fish scraps before snatching them up and marching over to the cat.

'There,' he says, throwing them to the ground. The cat looks disdainfully in the opposite direction, until the smell of the fish is too much even for him, and he approaches, whiskers twitching.

The man returns to where the woman is sitting, her back against the stone. His eyes take in its rough, grey surface, the hole through its centre, worn soft by time.

'May I?' he says awkwardly, indicating the ground beside her.

The woman tries not to let her surprise show. This is no ordinary visit, she thinks, but then, neither is it an ordinary time of year.

'Of course.'

With a grunt the man lowers himself to the ground, leans gingerly against the stone. 'I have never sat here before,' he murmurs after a time. 'I was afraid of this place as a child.'

The woman smiles quietly. 'And I.'

'Not any longer.'

'No.'

The man draws in a breath and places his hand on the stone's surface. His eyes flicker, something crossing their depths. 'I am glad it is still here,' he says, 'so much is missing.' He turns towards her in the dying light. 'It is the spaces I cannot grow accustomed to. My groomsmen, the mechanic, the boy from the brewery . . . All I can see are the gaps they've left. I don't see how the world can go on with so many parts missing.'

The woman meets his eyes. 'It goes on, Colonel Tremennor. It just does. The way it's always done.'

'You hate me, don't you?' His eyes are bright. 'You Roscarrows, you curse us, for what we've done over the years. You should now, you know. I deserve it.'

The woman rests her head against the stone. 'I can't speak for the others,' she sighs. 'Me . . . No. Maybe I did once, before Thomas. After, everything went out of me, except for a few scraps of feeling, and they died along with Frank. For a while, I had nothing left inside me at all. 'Til I felt her.' She looks down at the baby. 'Now, I only have space for what she brought, and that's hope, and love and sometimes worry, but certainly not hate for you, Colonel. I've no room for it.'

The baby is squirming. She kicks her legs in the swaddling, works an arm free and stretches it into the cold air, tiny fingers moving. Together, they look down at her.

'Did F . . .' the man's voice withers, 'was your husband aware he had a daughter?'

'No.' The woman closes her roughened hand around the child's small one. 'I didn't even know I was carrying when I received the news of him. I thought I might be too old, you see, though we'd prayed and prayed for another child, after Thomas.'

The man squeezes his eyes shut. 'I should have brought them back,' he says. 'I should have brought them home, rather than those damn plaques. You should not have been alone this Christmas.'

'I'm not alone. I have her,' she jogs the baby, 'and 'ee,' she nods to the cat, now licking the last scraps from the paper, 'and this place.' She looks up at the holly grove, its branches black against the fading sky. 'Frank always said that Enysyule was in his blood. I can't help feel there's something left of him and Thomas here.'

'This place . . .' the man repeats, staring into the darkness. Slowly his expression shifts, the shadows dropping away. 'You like it here?'

'Yes,' the woman gives him a sad smile. 'It brings me peace.'

'Then allow me to make you a Christmas gift, Mrs Roscarrow,' his smile shakes at the corners, 'a real one.'

He reaches down and scoops up a handful of earth from the base of the stone, flecked with dried holly leaves. Gently, he takes the woman's hand, and before she can protest, pours it onto her palm.

'Enysyule is yours,' he says. 'And hers. Merry Christmas.'

She closes her fingers around it, the gift of a valley in a handful of earth. I too try to hold it tight, but it is slipping away, sliding through my grip. I try to flex my hands, only to find that they are stiff with cold. I'm shivering, I realise, a deep trembling in my muscles. Drowsily I reach out, groping for the blanket on the armchair. My fingers close on leaves, thick and leathery and sharp. With a jolt, I open my eyes.

I'm in the clearing.

Shock courses through me as I blink, again and again, trying to wake up. Only, I'm already awake. What's more, I'm freezing. My pyjamas are cold and damp, my bare feet muddy. This isn't a dream. Above, the sky is pale grey with dawn. How long have I been out here?

I look around frantically, trying to find anything that might tell me how much time has passed, which century this is even, but it's like trying to find footing on ice. I remember the bronze discs, the fire . . . whatever came next slips away as I try to grasp it. When I close my eyes, I see a woman and a man, their backs against the stone, and Perrin . . .

'Perrin?' I call, opening my eyes. A shudder runs across my skin, like claws skittering down my neck, and it's only then I feel it. Something cold at my back. Slowly, I look up. The Perranstone towers over me, sombre as an owl in the dawn light. I could swear it meets my gaze. Trembling, my nails blue with cold, I raise a hand towards its surface.

The nearest tree rustles, twigs crack, and Perrin bounds from the undergrowth, yowling his head off. I've never been so happy to see him. His paws tramp across my legs, kneading the life back into them, he rubs his head on my chin, meowing repeatedly, as if scolding and comforting me at the same time. His fur is cold, and as I ruffle it, I see that there is frost on the ground. I shouldn't be out here, I think vaguely, words like *frostbite* and *hypothermia* drifting across my mind. I start to flex my numb fingers and toes, rubbing them clumsily, wincing as the blood tingles into the skin.

After a few minutes, I'm able to haul myself onto my knees, groaning at the stiffness in my muscles. At my side, Perrin has started to chatter angrily, the way I've seen him do at birds. Except there are no birds here, not even robins. I look around, following his gaze. He's staring fixedly at the stone.

I stagger to my feet, only for my legs to buckle under me. I kneel on the frost-rimed ground, trying to summon my strength. This is bad. Sleepwalking to the front door is one thing, but this . . . this is dangerous. *Desperate times*, a grim voice says at the back of my mind. *You asked the valley to show you something that would help. And it did.*

Gritting my teeth, I stand up again. This time I manage a few steps before my head spins, and I have to kneel before I fall over. Tears threaten my eyes. I need to get back to the cottage; need to get warm, quickly. At this rate it'll take me hours.

I force myself up again, determined to reach one of the holly trees so I can hold myself upright, when Perrin's chatter breaks off into a familiar chirrup of greeting. I turn my head, watching a figure walk out of the wood. *Not Alex,* I pray silently, *please, not now.* I make out a wax jacket, a bag over one shoulder, but no rushing of a dog through the undergrowth, and Perrin is quite at ease.

'Jess!' Jack calls when he sees me. For a second I almost laugh with relief, before I remember the state I'm in. How am I ever going to explain *this*?

'I was hoping you'd be at home,' he says, stepping into the clearing. Listen, I–' He stops, eyes travelling over my pyjamas, my bare feet, my chattering teeth. 'Jesus, what are you doing?'

If I had any blood to spare, it would be rushing to my cheeks. As it is, I force my numb lips into a smile. 'Morning stroll,' I tell him.

'You're not wearing any shoes!' Jack says disbelievingly. 'And are those . . . pyjamas?'

'Thermal walking suit,' I try to joke.

Jack rolls his eyes. 'Your lips are purple,' he says matter-of-factly, and drops his bag to take off his jacket. 'Put this on.'

I'm so cold, there's no way I'm going to argue. I stick my arms through the sleeves, hunching it around me, the fabric still warm from the heat of his body.

'Whatever it is you've been doing, you can tell me in a minute,' he says. 'Let's get into the warm first. I have some . . . news for you.' He slings the bag over his shoulder. 'If you've finished your morning stroll, that is.'

The thought of being helped along by Jack is so embarrassing that I clench my teeth, force myself to put one foot in front of the other. After a while, the movement begins to thaw my limbs, blood rushing back into my legs and feet. Jack is brooding on something as we walk; I catch him casting occasional, worried looks my way.

'What time is it?' I ask, when we're nearly at the ford. The morning is growing bright around us.

'What?' He frowns. 'Oh. About eight. Why? How long have you been out here?'

When I took the bronze discs out of the drawer it was still dark, can't have been more than half-past five in the morning. Nearly three hours, outdoors, in freezing weather . . . A shudder runs through me.

'I'm not sure,' I murmur.

Jack doesn't say anything, though his lips compress as if he's holding back words. Finally we walk the last few feet of the path towards the cottage. The front door stands ajar. Jack tuts when he sees it.

I'm too tired and cold to explain, just head straight for the fire that still smoulders sleepily. Sure enough, the bronze discs are glimmering in the ash of the hearth. I snatch them up, before Jack sees. For some reason, they feel private, personal. I shove them down the side of the armchair.

'Here,' Jack shakes out a blanket, tucks it around me. 'Get warm. Then we'll talk.'

I sit, huddled, while Jack stirs up the embers, gets the fire going, adding logs until it burns big and bright and hot. Furtively, I look down at the bronze discs.

'Frank John Roscarrow, Thomas Peter Roscarrow,' I whisper to myself.

'What?' asks Jack from the hob, where he stands over the kettle.

I blink round at him. 'Nothing. Are you making tea?'

'Yep. I'd make some breakfast as well but all I can find are tins of beans.'

'There's some bacon in the fridge,' I say defensively. 'And bread in the basket. I think.'

Jack bustles away, muttering to himself. I tuck my chin under the blanket, and close my eyes. What did I see, there in the clearing? The dream is as slippery as ever. A man, haunted by sorrow, a woman with nothing except the child in her arms, a whole valley contained within a handful of earth, a gift at Yuletide . . .

A smoky, savoury smell pulls me out of my thoughts. Bacon. I realise that I am ravenous. When Jack sees me looking, he hands over a mug of tea. A bacon sandwich – made with doorstop slices of bread – soon follows.

'I'm having one too,' he says, pulling a stool up to the hearth. 'Hope that's OK.'

'Of course.' I put down the tea and take an enormous bite of the sandwich, soft bread, crispy bacon, melted butter. 'This is amazing, thank you,' I mumble, mouth full. I'm about to attack it again when Jack catches my eye. I swallow. 'You want me to explain?'

'Well . . . it's none of my business,' he says. 'Though I will admit to being curious.'

I sigh, steeling myself for where this conversation might go. 'What would you say if I told you I sleepwalked there?'

He gives a short laugh. 'Well it would explain the pyjamas. I suppose I'd say that seems unlikely. It's a long way to walk without waking up.'

'I know, it's absurd,' I mutter, staring down at the plate. 'But my dreams, they're all about this place, about Enysyule. And they feel so *real*, as if the valley is trying to tell me—' I stop, blushing at how stupid it sounds. 'You'll think that's ridiculous,' I say, when he doesn't answer.

'I don't know.' There's a small frown between his dark brows. 'If we were anywhere else, I'd probably say yes, but . . .' He looks around at the cottage's walls, at its stone floor, worn by generations of feet. 'There's always been something different about this place. People in the village will pretend otherwise, but most of them are still afraid to come here.' He smiles crookedly. 'Old stories cling like tar.'

'So, you don't think I'm crazy?' I ask, trying to conceal the hope in my voice.

'Dunno about that,' he laughs, 'though I wouldn't be surprised if this place worked on you, somehow. Got tangled up in your thoughts.' He turns the mug in his hands. 'When I was at uni I had a friend who was studying geology. He was always going off into the wilderness, talking about places that . . . *remembered*. Didn't make him very popular with the tutors. But having grown up here, I always thought there might be something in it.'

He smiles at me and I smile back gratefully, feeling like someone has lifted a rock from my chest.

'I think I'm finally starting to warm up,' I tell him, and shrug out of his jacket. As I do, it occurs to me that I have no idea why he's here. His presence feels so comfortable, I didn't think to question it.

'Were you coming to see me?' I ask, handing the jacket over. His fingers brush mine, and abruptly I want to hold on, feel the warmth of his skin on mine. I sit back, looking down so that he doesn't see my face.

'Yes, I was.' He sounds serious, good humour dropping away as he retrieves his bag. 'I came over yesterday, but you weren't home. And I don't have your number, so I thought I'd stop by early today, try and catch you in.'

He comes back to the fire with a cardboard shoebox in his hands, secured with string.

'You're not going to like this,' he warns as he eases open the lid. I peer inside. There are a few small plastic trays, stamped with a logo. They're full of bright blue pellet-type things, which have spilled out, covering the bottom of the box.

'What the hell—?' I reach in, only for Jack to jerk the box away.

'Don't touch it,' he says.

'Why? What is that stuff?'

'It's rat poison. Highly toxic.'

I stare at him for a second. 'I don't . . . where did you get it?'

Carefully he puts the box on the floor. 'I was on my way over here yesterday, to ask how the meeting with Tremennor went. When I got to the clearing I saw Perrin. It was weird, he was just sitting there, staring at this dead mouse. He wasn't eating it or playing with it or anything. Then I saw that part of the undergrowth nearby had been trampled. I had a quick look there and' – he points to the box – 'found the first of those. Didn't take long to find the other three. Whoever put them down must been in a hurry.'

I shake my head at him. 'That doesn't make sense, why would anyone—?' I stop, an awful, cold suspicion trickling into my mind. A man, smiling out the words, *after all, how long do cats really live?*

'No,' I whisper, 'they wouldn't.' I meet Jack's eyes. His face is tense. I can tell he's thinking the same thing. *Yes, they would.*

I lurch up from the chair, feet tangling in the blanket. 'Perrin!'

Jack grabs my arm. 'Jess, he's fine,' he says quickly, 'he's too clever to fall for anything like that.'

'You don't understand!' I search around for my boots. 'He was ill last night, I knew there was something wrong with him.' All of a sudden I'm crying, tears spilling from my eyes. 'Those bastards,' I swear, 'if they've hurt him . . .'

I pull open the door, only to be greeted by a soft mewing noise. Perrin is sitting on the step, waiting to be let in. I scoop him up, bury my face in his cold fur, which smells like the frosty morning. He feels strong in my arms and full of energy, his eyes bright, not limp and listless any more. I carry him to the armchair by the fire where he jumps down, makes himself comfortable on my blanket. After a moment, I feel Jack squeeze my shoulder.

'He looks OK,' he says. 'I think we'd know if he wasn't.'

I nod, wipe my eyes on my sleeve. When I have my face back under control, I look up at him, at his bright hazel eyes creased in sympathy. 'Thank you, Jack.'

He smiles, and I feel it again, that charged space between our bodies. For an endless second I think he might move forward, might take my face in his hands, but then he's clearing his throat, stepping away.

'I'll – er – get rid of that for you,' he says hurriedly, nodding at the front step. There's a dead shrew there, one that *definitely* hasn't died of natural causes. Perrin must have brought it.

'Leave it,' I say, as he tears off a sheet of kitchen towel. 'And the box. I need them.'

He straightens up. 'What for?'

I feel a grim smile twist my lips. 'Evidence.'

The box trembles under my arm. I tighten my grip, in case I drop it. *Pull yourself together*, I tell myself, even though my insides feel like they're turning to foam. I pick up the heavy old door knocker, let it fall three times, booming and resonant.

A minute passes, two, and no one answers. I hammer again, louder than before. Silence. I've come all this way, worked myself up for a fight, all for nothing. What if Tremennor can see me? I suddenly wonder. What if he's watching me through some hidden camera, laughing at me from the safety of his office? I put the box down on the front step and sneak around the side of the house to investigate. All the doors are locked, windows closed tightly against the cold. He must truly be out. I find myself standing hopelessly by the back door, staring down at the fire pit and the walled garden where Alex and I first— I cut that thought off before it goes anywhere. Do I wait, or try again later? Leaving now feels like defeat . . .

I've made up my mind to wait when something brown flashes across my vision. I turn, just in time to see Maggie streak out of the lane that leads to the coach house, heading straight for the front door.

'Shit!' I break into a run, throwing myself around the side of the house. I sprint down the gravel path, cursing under my breath for being such an idiot. Maggie has pawed the lid from the cardboard box, has her head inside it.

'Maggie!' I yell, racing up towards her. The unexpectedness of my appearance breaks her concentration and she looks around, ears quirked. The poisoned shrew is held between her jaws.

'Drop it!' I command, my voice shaky. 'Maggie, drop it!' She only stares at me with her quick eyes, prances away when I try to reach for the shrew, like it's a game. 'Maggie!' I yell again, running after her, only to crash into a figure coming round the other side of the hedge.

'Jess!' Alex says. 'What—?'

'Tell her to drop it,' I gasp, pointing to the dog.

He looks utterly confused, glancing at Maggie. 'Drop . . . what are you talking about?'

'Alex, tell her to drop it! Now!'

He must sense the panic in my voice, because he doesn't argue, just turns away to where Maggie stands, delighted by this game.

'Maggie,' he says in a commanding tone, 'drop.'

She ducks and skitters, as though about to run away. When he says it more forcefully, she opens her jaw, reluctantly lets the dead shrew drop to the ground. Instantly I dash forward and snatch it up. It's disgusting, coated in warm drool, but I'm so relieved I don't care. I march back to the box and shove it inside, tuck everything safely under my arm, though Maggie rushes and leaps, wanting to play.

'Jess,' Alex says, coming towards me. 'What the hell's going on? What are you doing here?'

I take a steadying breath. 'I came to see your father. About his latest trick.'

Alex's face closes. 'What are you talking—?'

'Don't pretend you don't know,' I cut him off, furious. At least with Roger, our enmity is mutual, has clear lines, but with Alex . . . 'You're probably the one who put them there. Running errands for Daddy, as usual.'

'Look, whatever's got you worked up this time, it's nothing to do with me.'

'Really?' I ask sarcastically. 'Then you can't explain this?' I thrust the box into his arms.

He lifts off the lid, face creasing with revulsion at the sight of the dead, mangled shrew amongst the blue pellets. 'What the hell? You were going to leave this on the front step? What's wrong with you?'

'No, I was going to show it to your father. And I was going to inform him that if he *ever* tries to kill my cat again, I'll call the police.'

Alex's face pales. 'What?'

I point to the box. 'What is that stuff? You tell me.'

He peers down again, looking at the contents properly for the first time. 'Rat poison.' he murmurs after a few seconds, looking ill.

'I thought you'd recognise it. *Someone* left it scattered through the woods around Enysyule, I'm guessing in the hope that it would kill Perrin.' I meet his eyes. 'As far as I know, there's only one person who would benefit from that.'

Alex shakes his head, speechless, and for the first time I realise his shock might be genuine.

'No,' he says, 'he wouldn't, that's . . . crazy. I walk Maggie through those woods almost every day.' He stops, looks around for the dog. She looks up at him patiently, tongue lolling.

'Now do you see why I wanted her to drop it?' I say, some of the anger leaving my voice. 'If she'd eaten it she would have been poisoned. Luckily Perrin was too smart to.'

Alex bends to ruffle Maggie's ears, peer into her eyes. 'How do you know it was my father?' he asks, without looking around.

'Who else would it have been?'

He has no answer to that. I can see he's thinking hard, trying to find some way to argue back.

'You can't prove anything,' he says eventually, not meeting my eyes. 'You have no way to prove it was him.'

'I'll bet you any money there's a half-empty bag of this stuff somewhere in the house,' I say. When he doesn't reply, a bitter laugh escapes me. 'Whatever, Alex. Just pass on the message, OK?'

I turn away, energy draining from me. I want to leave the ugliness and conflict of this place behind, want to be back in the quiet, enveloping valley, with the fireplace and Perrin and nothing except dreams to disturb me.

'Wait!' Alex catches at my sleeve. 'Can't we forget about all this? We were having fun, you and me, before any of this happened.'

'You lied to me.' I pull away. 'How can you even pretend you care?'

'I thought I was doing the right thing. Jess, you don't know my father, what he can be like . . . please, let me try and make this up to you.'

'Make it up to me? Jesus, Alex, this isn't like missing a birthday or cancelling a date—'

'I know, I know,' he reaches for my sleeve again, 'but there must be something I can do. Please. I feel awful about everything. And . . . I miss you.'

I look at his hand, caught in the fabric of my coat, his eyes, raised hopefully to mine. 'There's one thing you can do.'

'Yes? Whatever it is, just tell me.'

'You can help me prove your father's lying about Enysyule,' I say bluntly. 'Whatever evidence he has, I need to see it.'

'Jess.' He lets his hand fall from my coat. 'I can't.'

'You can. You know what he's doing is wrong.'

Alex looks into my eyes, and for an instant, I think he's going to agree. 'It's not my problem,' he mumbles, stepping away. 'I'll tell Dad you were here.'

Then he's calling for Maggie, hurrying away towards the house, his head bent to his chest like a man who is weathering a storm.

★　　★　　★

Sometimes, human minds get trapped in the warp and weft of life. They see only what they expect to see, not what could be, or what has been or even what is. But the human heart is a landscape of its own; and what appears to be rock might melt in the ferocity of a storm, until it is as soft as river sand.

★　　★　　★

The feeling of exhaustion soon turns into a blocked nose and a raw throat. My eyes feel hot and dry in my head, my cheeks burning. I don't make tea; drink cup after cup of water from the tap. It's cold as stone, so cold it hurts my teeth, and still, I feel thirsty. Eventually I realise that this is the price I'm going to have to pay for my sleepwalking adventure: a horrible cold.

I spend the night shivering under the blankets, sweat soaking the back of my neck. The fever ebbs after a day or two, leaving me wiped out. My body is taking its time to shake the illness, as if it knows that a life-changing experience is waiting, only a few days away. On Monday I will have to face Roger Tremennor, face the terrifying prospect of losing this place. But for now, as much as it can be, Enysyule is mine. Inside these thick, stone walls Perrin and I are protected, safe and dry and snug. As one day slips into two, into three, I stop seeing the cottage's flaws. Instead I wrap myself in its character, in its timelessness, thick and comforting as an eiderdown.

I start to clear out the spare room, dragging away dustsheets that haven't been moved for years, opening boxes, unearthing treasures and trash: stacks of old art periodicals, a broken chair, a battered, empty suitcase, a basket that looks suspiciously like the one carried by the woman in my dream . . .

In one corner, I find a rough wooden crate, filled with what looks like bundles of yellowing paper. As I move it, something glimmers amongst the newsprint, catching my attention. I reach down, fingers pushing aside crinkling paper until I touch glass, thin and fragile. I lift the object free. It's a bauble. I've never seen one like it before. As a child, our decorations were a hodge-podge of felt snowmen and plastic icicles, mismatched tinsel and a wooden star for the top; a treasured gift from my grandmother in Istanbul that had seen better days. This one, on the other hand, is delicate and beautiful.

I brush the dust from it. Deep green glass, etched with a pattern that I can't quite make out, leaves or snow. Gold clings to the surface, sparkling in the light from the lamps as I turn it this way and that. I place the bauble back in its paper with a smile, feeling something I haven't felt for years: a rush of excitement for Christmas.

Whatever happens, I decide, whatever Tremennor throws at me, I *will* see Christmas in at Enysyule. For some reason, that decision makes me feel better. And although my throat is still sore, and my nose runs and my head aches, I start to write again. It's as if, for these few days, I can leave the real world behind. I wrap myself in my biggest cardigan, pull on thick socks beneath my pyjamas, and let my imagination loose. I write about a land of rocks and spirits, of creatures made from ice and fur, a world that can only be reached once a year, by peering through the centre of a stone . . .

Of course Perrin helps, usually by knocking my tissues to the floor, by walking over the keyboard and standing in my way when he thinks it's time for his dinner. He's as talkative and stubborn as ever, and yet, it seems that he's slowing down somehow. He doesn't leave the house so much these days. Perhaps it's the cold weather. His walk is stiffer, and he hasn't tried to attack my mouse for weeks.

One night, beside the fire, I heave him off the seat of the chair and onto my lap. He doesn't protest, only flexes his paws into the wool of my jumper and begins a low, drowsy purr. I stroke his head, wishing that people's ancient fears about the valley were true; that there was something here, older and more savage than humans, something that would protect this place ferociously, with tooth and claw if it had to. As I smooth a hand down Perrin's back, I notice a scattering of white through his fur, like pale snow. *Just his winter coat*, I tell myself, squashing down a tremor of worry.

Sunday afternoon creeps into Sunday evening, bringing a sense of dull dread I haven't felt since school, nursing the final dregs of the weekend to make it last. Tomorrow, Tremennor and his solicitor will swagger into Michaela's office, knowing that they have us beaten. It's maddening, that he can take Enysyule from me with something as flimsy as a signed piece of paper. All I have to retaliate with are dreams and stories. They may be strong enough to usurp my sleep, make me walk the length of the valley in the dead of night, but they will wither to nothing the moment I try to wield them against Tremennor. *I'm sorry, Thomasina*, I think as I lie in bed. *I tried.*

My outdoor clothes feel uncomfortable, after four days of pyjamas. I don't bother with looking smart this time, just wrap up extra warm for my walk to the village. I'm still not completely well. I look pale and worried and tired; no state to go into battle. Fittingly the day too is damp and chill and grey, mist hanging low through the valley, surrounding the stone. Carefully, I walk past it and step over the boundary, into the wood. After several days isolated from the rest of the world, the change is dramatic. I feel small and exposed and very alone.

I haven't walked far when I feel a frantic buzzing in my pocket. My phone. I haven't had a signal for so long, I'd almost forgotten it existed. I pull it out. There are a couple of missed calls, one from my agent, one from Mum, and a message. My fingers tighten around the plastic. It's from Alex. I tell myself I should probably just delete it straight away, but eventually the curiosity is too much.

I open it to find that there are no words, just a picture, sent in the early hours of this morning. A photo of a document; a single typewritten page, concluded by a signature. Hands trembling, I enlarge the image, stare at it in disbelief for a few breathless seconds, before breaking into a run.

I race through the woods, forgetting about my weak muscles, my sore throat and the fact I can't breathe through my nose. My boots land in mud and leaves, splattering my jeans. I veer away from the path to the village, taking the one towards the boatyard instead, following the stream as it rushes towards the river, throaty with winter rain. *Please be in*, I pray as I run, *please someone be in.*

By the time I cross the bridge below Lanford and stagger up the hill into the village, I feel like I'm about to collapse from over-exertion but I don't care. Something has burst into life in my chest; hope, as bright and unstoppable as a spark from a flint. I just hope I'm not too late. Through the windows of Michaela's office I can see her and Liza sitting at a desk, the solicitor leaning over them. Roger Tremennor toys with a paperweight to one side. Michaela is staring grimly at a document before her, pen in hand. Gasping, I grab for the handle and lurch through the door.

'Don't—' I try to say before the words dissolve into a cough. All four of them look up in surprise, taking in my bright red face, my mud-splashed jeans and bedraggled hair. Liza recovers first, and hurries to fetch me a glass of water.

'Ah,' I hear the solicitor say as I gulp it down, 'the tenant. Miss Price, wasn't it? I'm afraid there's really nothing for you to do—'

'Have you signed anything?' I interrupt, staring at Michaela. I must look a mess, my eyes flooding, an empty glass clutched in my hand. After a few seconds, she shakes her head.

'No,' she says. 'I wanted to wait until you were here. Why?'

Wordlessly I pull out my phone, the photograph Alex sent me clear upon it. 'Is this your proof?' I ask Tremennor, holding the phone towards him.

He frowns and squints at the screen. I watch as his face changes, the blood rushing up his neck, and I have to snatch the phone away before he can grab it.

'That is a private document!' he hisses. 'Where the hell did you get it?'

'You haven't answered the question.' I keep my voice level. 'Is it your proof? The document where Thomasina says she's a tenant?'

'Jess,' Michaela demands, standing up. 'What's going on?'

I step out of Roger Tremennor's reach and unzip my bag. Inside is the sketchbook I retrieved from Mel only minutes before. 'This was Thomasina's,' I tell them all, opening the creaking pages. 'I found it at the cottage. It's full of her drawings.'

The solicitor snorts a laugh. 'I'm sorry, what is the point of this? We're not here to look at old doodles.'

I ignore him, turn swiftly to the final sketch in the book. 'When did Thomasina supposedly sign that document?' I ask Tremennor.

He stares at me silently, lips compressed into a tight line.

'I believe,' Mr Mitchell intervenes, 'it was the month before Ms Roscarrow passed. May the twentieth, if I'm not mistaken?' Although his voice is smooth, his composure is starting to fray at the edges. He glances at Tremennor with a look that clearly says *what the hell haven't you told me?*

'Yes,' Tremennor agrees stiffly. 'The twentieth.'

I put the sketchbook on the desk and swivel it around for them to see. The drawing itself is almost impossible to make out, just a collection of thin, shaky lines, but to me, the subject is obvious. It's a picture of the Perranstone, as it might look from above: a circle surrounded by dark trees, the edges dissolving into smoke. In the bottom right corner, there's a signature and a date. It's barely legible.

'If she could hardly write on May the eighteenth,' I level at Tremennor, 'explain how she signed this so clearly on the twentieth?' I expand the picture on the phone, and lay it next to the drawing. The signatures are almost embarrassingly different. 'You'll understand if I have some questions about this document's . . . authenticity.'

For a second, no one moves.

'That's poppycock,' Roger bursts, his voice more than a little strangled. 'I've never seen that book before. You could easily have made it up.'

'What, the same way that you made up her signature?' I retort. 'Another one of your ploys, like trying to poison Perrin?'

His face flames red. 'Now look here!'

'What is going on?' the solicitor tries to interrupt.

'I know it was you!' I can't stop my voice from rising. 'Don't even try to deny it!'

'It's not my fault if you have a problem with vermin.'

'You b—'

'Quiet!' Michaela booms, shocking us all into silence. She heaves a heavy breath. 'Thank you. Firstly, I can confirm that sketchbook was Thomasina's. I saw her with it many times. Secondly,' she opens a ring binder on the desk and begins to leaf through it. 'Don't forget that Thomasina also signed an agreement with *us* in April of this year.' She pulls a thick document from a plastic wallet and hurriedly licks her thumb to turn the pages. 'It should provide us with a good comparison. Ah . . .'

I watch every tiny movement on her face as she scrutinises the signature line of the contract. For one, heart-stopping moment, I think she's about to shake her head at me; then her lips twitch, her eyes crease, and with a barely contained smile, she lays the paper next to the book and the phone.

As one, we crane our necks to see.

'I'm afraid I agree with Miss Pike, Roger,' Michaela says coolly, smiling sidelong at me. 'Your proof is looking more than a little . . . fictitious.'

The noise of a radio drifts out from one of the boatyard sheds. I make a beeline for it, the cold, damp air of the river stinging my lungs. I stop in the doorway, gripping a stitch in my side. Jack is working at a bench, the sleeves of his jumper rolled up to the elbow, planing down a plank of wood. My throat feels stuck together. It takes three attempts before I'm able to summon up enough moisture to croak his name.

His smile of surprise soon drops into concern when he sees the state of me, breathless and bright-eyed with emotion.

'Jess?' He puts down the plane and comes forwards, wiping his hands on a rag. 'What is it? What's wrong?'

'We did it,' I say, half-laughing, even as the tears start up again. 'We did it, Jack. Michaela and Liza and I . . .'

'Did what?' he says urgently.

'We proved that Tremennor doesn't have a case.' I can hardly believe the words, even as I say them. 'He's dropping his claim to Enysyule!'

Before I know what's happening, Jack has swept me into a hug, lifting me off the ground. I grip his shoulders in return, engulfed in the scent of fresh wood and old wool, soap and smoke clinging to his hair and skin. He sets me down and for one, aching moment our bodies are close, faces closer. Then he's turning away, his eyes, the colour of autumn, creased in a laugh.

'Come on!' he says. 'We have to tell Mel. He won't believe it!'

That afternoon turns into one of the best I can remember since arriving in Lanford. Mel breaks out the brandy again, this time in celebration. He and Jack put work on hold for a few hours, and together, in their kitchen with its view over the grey-green River Lan, we eat and talk and laugh, warmed by the wood burner, by spirits, by a flood of relief after weeks of worry. I tell them what happened in Michaela's office; how Tremennor retracted his offer, muttering something about a 'miscommunication', how even the solicitor had stared daggers at his back when they left.

'So, young Jessie.' Mel says, his face flushed. 'That mean you're here to stay?'

'It does,' I laugh, raising my glass to clink with his.

A guardian and protector for Enysyule for as long as Perrin shall live. The words of the agreement come back to me as I drink. They create a tiny fissure in my happiness, like a single cloud in a flawless sky when I remember the white hairs scattered through Perrin's black coat. I push it away, focus instead on listening to Mel.

'. . . only two weeks away, you know,' he says.

'What's is?'

'Christmas! Yuletide. Important time of year, round these parts.' He swallows down the remainder of his brandy, pours a little more.

Jack opens the wood burner to throw a few more logs in. The flames catch upon the amber liquid in my glass. *Flames in the darkness*, images fill my mind between breaths, *light on stone, voices raised in song and holly leaves, dark as a secret pool, berries red as blood . . .*

'What happens here, at Yuletide?' I hear myself asking.

'What *doesn't* happen?' Mel leans forward, glass cupped in his hands. 'The nights grow darker and darker, daylight shorter as the sun wears himself out an' the old year is worn to a ravelling. Then, it's time for Montol.' He takes a sip of brandy, casts a sly look my way.

'And what is Montol?' I ask dutifully.

'The solstice,' Jack says, before his grandfather can. 'The longest night and the shortest day. There's always a party.'

'Like when the Christmas lights were switched on?'

Mel snorts. 'You call that a party? *Montol* is a party.' His eyes widen as they meet mine. 'There's music, an' lanterns, and the geeze-dancing, and folk go dressed in masks and tatters—'

'It's a night of misrule. A night where anything can happen.' Jack says, closing the stove. 'Some people work on their costumes for months.'

'Even you?' I tease, remembering his lack of fancy dress on Halloween.

'Even me,' he nods with mock-solemnity, 'rules are rules.'

'It sounds wonderful.' I laugh. 'I had better find something to wear.'

'So, you'll be staying?' Jack asks softly, meeting my gaze as he takes the chair beside mine. 'At Enysyule? You'll come to Montol?'

'Yes,' I say, remembering his arms around me, the heat of his cheek against mine as he lifted me from the floor. 'I'm staying.' When the silence grows a beat too long, I knock back the rest of my brandy, wince as it burns my throat. 'My family are coming down from London for Christmas too. My mum and my sister and her husband. But the cottage is such a mess still, and I've barely even *started* on the spare room.'

'Sounds like you need a helping hand,' Mel says nonchalantly, 'someone to pitch to it.'

Jack laughs at his grandfather's lack of subtlety. 'I'd be happy to help, Jess,' he says, over my protests. 'Just let me know what you need.'

I walk back through the darkening winter wood with feet far lighter than they were just hours before. In the chill air, my face glows warm, the smell of woodsmoke and brandy hovering around me. Perrin is waiting for me on the doorstep of the cottage; I see his mouth moving in a meow before I can hear it, as though he is calling for me to hurry, anxious for news. I scoop him up into my arms, dance him around the kitchen, telling him everything that's happened, that his home is safe again. When I put him down he settles in his favourite spot, giving me one, slow blink as if to say *well, of course I knew it would all work out in the end*.

That night we celebrate with a special dinner: fresh mackerel that I picked up from the fishermen. I cook mine just as they told me to, over the hot coals of the fire, until the cottage is filled with the scent of sea and wood. As the winter night deepens outside, I try to imagine London, on this cold December evening. It seems impossible that even now, crowds of people are pushing along Oxford Street for late night Christmas shopping, chatting on the escalators, fogging up the windows of the buses that start-stop through the streets, while I sit here in the quiet, eating fish hot from the flames.

It makes me smile at how far I've come from the young woman who ran away from the city, a pair of dusty plimsolls on her feet and a mind full of unnecessary things. This place has changed me. On the threadbare rug, Perrin is busy washing his face, and as I watch him, my heart is filled to bursting with gratitude, to be right here, at Enysyule, in this moment.

★　★　★

The wild hunt rides across the winter skies, wheeling with the stars, plunging with the rain. The old year – their quarry – is flagging and each leap lasts a day, each stumble a night. How long precisely doesn't matter, for the hunters and the hunted both know what humans so often forget: that time is not the only measure of being.

★　★　★

Evergreen. The scent infiltrates my dreams, pulling me gently from sleep. I open my eyes to darkness, expecting it to have faded, but no: the powerful, resiny scent of freshly cut branches is filling the room, as though someone has covered the bed in boughs of holly and fir. I sit up, breathing deeply, wondering whether it's a trick of the house. No, it's too strong for that. I slide from the bed and place my feet on the boards. My skin is tingling all over as I stand up slowly, not wanting to disturb ... whatever it is that's happening.

The scent is stronger on the tiny landing, almost overwhelming as I walk down the stairs into the darkness of the main room, with its sleeping red fire. Beside the hearth sits the wooden box of decorations I found in the spare room. I brought it down before I went to bed, excited to get the cottage cleaned up and ready for the Christmas holidays.

There's a spark of green as I approach. I know exactly what it is. Carefully, I kneel and lift the glass bauble from its cocoon of paper. At first I'm afraid to look at it too closely, remembering what happened last time I gazed into one of Enysyule's secrets. But the scent of holly and evergreen is rising all around me, my skin is prickling with the approach of something I cannot name, and I know that I have no choice.

I raise the ornament to my eye. It spins gently in my grip, something shifting in its depths. A figure, moving about a room that looks very much like the one behind me. A woman, young, standing at the kitchen table before a pile of freshly cut holly. She turns, picking up a pair of shears and I catch a flash of her eyes, flecked hazel. She looks familiar, like someone I knew a long time ago. Her dark brows are drawn together in a frown of concentration as she carefully snips a sprig from a branch of holly. Absent-mindedly, she sings to herself.

'*Ha'n kelynn yw an kynsa a'n gwydh oll y'n koes . . .*'

She lowers the shears, looks down at herself critically, at the old woollen jumper, the thick trousers cinched around her waist with a man's belt. Her only other clothes are over-alls or faded summer dresses that look odd with her stout boots. Except for the new blue dress that hangs upstairs, the polished shoes. *That* outfit is for a special occasion, a special person.

Christmas Day. It will be the first they spend together at the cottage, she's decided. No matter that they're not official yet. Two days leave at Yuletide are too precious to waste on her family at the boatyard, enduring their disapproving glances, their hushed whispers about him, a foreign soldier from far away with no home of his own. She smiles mischievously, snipping another sprig from the holly, imagining the faces of the people in Lanford when they hear about the wedding.

'Brodzki,' she whispers to herself, savouring the pattern of it on her lips, secret and sweet as black-market sugar, 'Mrs Thomasina Brodzki.'

Gathering up a handful of holly, she moves to the huge, old dresser in the corner. From one of the drawers she takes out a cardboard box, and from it lifts a beautiful, blown-glass ornament, gilded with the pattern of a star. A gift for her future husband, to remind him of Christmas in his homeland. She turns it in the light. It feels like little to offer, to make up for all he has lost. But, she decides, it will be worth it, to see his smile on Christmas Eve.

She starts to arrange the holly boughs, eyes falling on the bronze plaques that hang on the wall, bearing the names of a father and a brother she never knew. A wave of sorrow rushes through her as she tucks a sprig of holly behind the photograph of her mother, placed on the top shelf, near the plaques.

If they were here, all of them, would they disapprove? They wouldn't want her to be alone, she is sure of that. Anyway, she won't be going anywhere; Piotr knows that Enysyule will be his home too. He already has the approval of the only other person who matters.

She glances over her shoulder at the armchair. It is occupied by a black, furry lump, fast asleep, tucked into a ball.

'You're lucky the fishermen still care for you, you know,' she says idly. 'Without them, you'd have to catch your own supper, like a real cat.'

The cat opens one yellow eye and stares out from beneath his paw. With a laugh, the young woman turns to place a bough of holly on the top shelf. As she does, a change comes across her face; her eyes widen, turn distant, and her fingers tighten about the holly leaves, despite the cruel spines. Only when the blood starts to well does she come back to herself. She stares down as a droplet splashes onto the flagstones, scattering the ash like rain.

'No,' she breathes. The holly falls to the floor, forgotten as she runs for the stairs, taking them two at a time, bursting into what she still thinks of as her mother's bedroom. The wireless stands on the windowsill, the best place to catch the airwaves, and she scrabbles to turn the dials, not caring that she leaves blood on them.

Paris, Moscow, Warsaw ... Piotr's country; the two of them have sat like children here, trying to pick up scraps from his homeland. But the radio is crackling and unsettled and every turn of the dial produces the slow, endless hiss of static.

'Come on,' she begs, searching for the local frequencies, for an announcement, a bulletin, a warning, 'please!'

There's nothing, and the sense of dread only gets stronger. From the pit of her stomach, she can feel it calling her ... Giving up on the radio, she races down the stairs, slipping in her much-darned socks, and crams her feet into the work boots that stand by the door, still wet from her day in the fields.

'Please,' she finds herself whispering, like a prayer, like an incantation, 'please, please.'

She flings open the door, gets one glimpse of Perrin's face as he looks up in alarm. Then she is running, down the path, away from the cottage. She doesn't bother with a torch; she knows these paths as well as her own skin and the night is clear, the moon bulging like an eye above the valley. She takes the ford at a run, leaps over the high, winter stream and races on, to answer the summons.

The holly trees rise at the end of the path. Only a few hours ago, she wandered among them, her old friends, taking what branches they offered, the way she does every year. Now, they look dark and unknowable and the blood still wells from where their leaves have cut her.

She bursts into the clearing. The Perranstone is waiting, blind and grey. She is not scared of it. It knows her. It has taken hairs from her head and salt from her tears, has heard her chatter at playtime, and supported her back during afternoon naps on hot summer days . . .

'What?' she cries to it now, striking its surface. 'What is it? Tell me!' Her blood leaves smears across the pale, silent stone. 'Please,' she gasps, trying to catch her breath. 'Please, say he's safe.'

Her nerves fizz. She can't hear anything except her own breathing. Then, distantly, something else: the sound of an engine, drifting down from the sky. It's enough to make her look up in astonishment. She has never heard an aircraft here before. There is something about the valley that keeps the noise of the world out. She strains her ears. Yes, an aircraft engine, she's sure, even if it sounds wrong. It's stuttering and coughing, the noise of a machine pushed to breaking. It comes closer and closer. She stares up, into the circle of sky above the clearing, until at last she sees something.

Four years of paranoia are almost enough to make her drop to the ground, or run for cover, but her hands seem welded to the stone, and in the bright moonlight, she can see enough of the markings to know it isn't an enemy plane. The noise of the ailing engines is almost deafening now. Only one propeller is spinning, she realises, and clouds of black smoke are billowing from the engine. It shouldn't be here, it's flying too low, miles from the nearest base, and there is nowhere to land among the river creeks and steep hills of Lanford. Unless . . .

The instant the plane passes over the stone, she knows. No one would fly here, in a plane that could crash at any moment, with nowhere safe to land, unless they had to. Unless they knew it was their last chance to look upon the place where they had hoped to build a life, where the person they love lies sleeping, or dreaming by the fire; a final glimpse of Enysyule, before the end . . .

'Piotr!' the young woman screams, staring up at the plane desperately, straining to make out the cockpit through the smoke. She screams his name again and again, though she knows he won't be able to hear, knows at best he'll be able to see a small figure, an upturned face, beside a grey stone.

The plane stutters and whines and begins to drop rapidly. It is flying out of sight, being swallowed by the holly trees, and she runs towards them, trying to follow, even though she knows it is hopeless. The black leaves scratch at her arms and push her away, until she falls, back into the clearing, beside the stone, her sobs mingling with the sound of a fading engine.

From the other side of the clearing, something comes running towards her. She doesn't raise her head, she can't, not even when a paw is pressed against her tear-slicked cheek . . .

Perrin standing on my lap, one paw raised to my face. He smells of the night, cold air clinging to him, as though he has just come racing in from outside. As soon as I focus on him, he drops back to both feet, but doesn't move away. I take a deep breath, wiping away the tears that have filled my eyes.

I lower the bauble back into its nest of paper. Thomasina never married. Of that I'm certain. I always assumed she was a recluse, preferred living a solitary existence. Perhaps that wasn't the case. Perhaps she was never able to share her life with anyone else.

Except Perrin. I stroke his head as he sits before me, tail swishing anxiously, as though he remembers last week's sleepwalking escapade. At least this time it's only my feet that have gone numb. Wearily I climb the stairs to bed. The scent of evergreen has faded, I realise, as I drag the covers back over me. Perrin settles near my feet, and soon, comforted by his presence, I fall into a deep, dreamless sleep.

✳   ✳   ✳

News travels fast in a place like Lanford, and over the course of the week, Enysyule has a steady flow of callers. Michaela shows up one lunchtime with a camp bed and a blow-up mattress, so I can sleep my family comfortably when they visit. Liza sends over a stack of spare bed linen and towels. Even the notorious local handywoman, Mrs Hesketh, finally makes an appearance to do some work on the plumbing. She brings her grandson with her to help, a silent young man of about fifteen who flushes bright red whenever he's addressed. Mrs Hesketh, on the other hand, is cantankerously good-natured, and stomps into the bathroom before I even tell her what the problem is. I watch as she unscrews something from the boiler and chucks it over her shoulder.

'Hand us that wassacum, Tobe,' she calls to her grandson.

It's as if the people of the village have been waiting to see what would happen with Tremennor, before making their move. Eventually I ask her what she thinks about it all.

'Course we knew he was fibbing,' she tells me brusquely. 'But then, these are hard times, and there's not many would've blamed Michaela for taking that cash.'

I don't ask how she knows the – presumably confidential – details of the business with Tremennor; this is Lanford, after all.

The only person I don't hear from is Alex. I think about texting him at least a dozen times, to thank him for doing the right thing, even though it must have put him in a difficult position with his father. At the last minute, though, I always remember his words that day at the manor – *can't we forget about all this? We were having fun, you and me, before any of this happened* – and delete the message. I don't want to get involved again. Better to leave things where they are, call it quits. Especially when there's one visitor I always look forward to seeing . . .

Jack shows up one afternoon, brandishing a pot of paint and a couple of rollers.

'Thought these might be useful,' he announces, before his eyes stray to the table, to the laptop open there. 'Sorry, you're writing, didn't mean to interrupt—'

'No, it's OK,' I say hurriedly as he turns away. 'I mean, I was about to take a break, if you wanted a cup of tea?'

Perrin is hogging the armchair as usual, so we sit opposite each other at the kitchen table. There's a shaving of wood caught in the dark curls of his hair. I resist the urge to reach across and pull it free.

'Jess,' he says, so suddenly that I blush, hoping my thoughts aren't written all over my face. 'Can I ask you something, about Montol?'

'Montol?' I try to sound casual. 'The winter solstice party?'

'Yes. It's kind of a big deal round here. For one night, this whole place goes topsy-turvy.'

'I find that hard to imagine,' I laugh. 'When is it?'

'The twenty-first. This Saturday.' Jack puts down his mug, looking serious. 'Jess, I wanted to ask you whether you might, possibly . . .'

Yes! I'm already saying in my head, *Jack, I'd love to go with you!*

'. . . consider going with my grandfather.'

The words clunk into place in my mind.

'Sorry?' I manage to ask, wondering if I misheard. 'You mean, go with Mel?'

Jack nods, looking down into the mug. 'He hasn't been to Montol since Grandma Phyllis died. Don't think he can bring himself to go alone. And he won't listen to me. But . . . I have this feeling he won't be able to say no to you.' He looks at me, a sad frown creasing his brows. 'You've been good for him, Jess. The last few weeks he's been more alive than I've seen him in years. I don't know,' he smiles ruefully, 'I think your quarrel put some fire back in his belly.'

I return Jack's smile, trying not to let my disappointment show.

'Of course I'll go with him,' I say. 'It's the least I can do.'

His smile broadens. 'Thanks.' He reaches out and squeezes my hand. 'It'll mean the world to him.'

I look into his eyes only for my nose to betray me. I have to snatch my hand from his, grab a tissue before I sneeze explosively.

'Although if you're still not well . . .' Jack says with concern.

'No, I'm fine,' I blink watering eyes. 'Or I will be by Saturday, I promise.'

As he puts on his jacket, I work up the courage to ask him a different question.

'Jack, was Thomasina ever . . . engaged or anything?' I ask. 'When she was younger?'

'Thomasina? Engaged?' Jack makes a face, pulling a hat over his hair. 'Doubt it. She didn't have much time for other people. Certainly didn't suffer fools gladly. Why do you ask?'

'Just wondering.'

'Still having dreams?' he says shrewdly.

'Yes,' I admit. 'Don't worry though, there haven't been more adventures outside.' I hesitate, steeling myself to confide in him. 'It's strange. They're getting stronger, and at the same time, I don't mind them any more. They make me feel sort of . . . connected.' I grimace. 'That doesn't make any sense, does it?'

I expect him to laugh in return, but he doesn't.

'This is going to sound a bit odd,' he sighs, as though he can't quite believe what he's about to say. 'But I think this place is different in winter. I think it's always had something to do with the Yuletide. I mean, it's in the name, *enys*, it means something isolated, or secret, and *yule*, well . . .' he shrugs meaningfully. 'If someone was naming it today, they'd probably call it Yule Cottage.'

I stare at him. He's ordinarily so rational and sardonic, I can't tell whether he's joking.

'Do you think it's anything to do with . . .?' I nod my head across the valley, in the direction of the clearing, where the Perranstone waits, silent and watchful.

'I've no idea,' Jack murmurs. I realise we're standing close, as though there was someone to overhear us. 'It would make sense though. That stone has been there for thousands of years. Long before Christmas was Christmas.'

All at once, a chirruping noise makes us both leap out of our skin. Together we look over to see Perrin, peering around the armchair at us.

'I think he might agree with me,' Jack laughs.

'Thanks for coming over,' I tell him by the door. 'And tell Mel that I'd be honoured to go with him to Montol.'

'Thank you, Jess.' He doesn't turn away, worrying at something in the deep pocket of his coat. 'I . . .' he clears his throat and pulls out a small newspaper-wrapped cone. 'I saw these in town. Thought you might like them.'

He hands them over. Surprised, I look down at the paper in my hands. Within, there's a posy of white flowers, their yellow stamens tiny as stars, among deep green leaves, almost as dark as holly.

'What are they?' I ask, but Jack's already striding away down the path, waving over his shoulder.

Beaming, I look down at the flowers again. A little tag is tied to the stems with string.

Hellebores: it says in neat handwriting, *Christmas roses.*

As the days draw towards Montol, a feverish mood starts to spread through Lanford. I see that Jack and Mel are right; the festival looks set to be a grand affair. Two days before,

Michaela and Liza hold their Christmas party, cramming people into their tiny office for an afternoon of mince pies, mulled wine and merriment, until the windows are too steamed up to see, and there's little point in anyone going back to work.

Through the high-spirited chatter and Christmas songs blaring out of computer speakers, I see Geoff, standing on his own, staring at a map of the surrounding countryside on the wall. I make my way across.

'Hello, Geoff,' I say hesitantly, not wanting to disturb his reverie.

His face brightens. 'Miss Pike. How are you?'

'Much better than the last time I saw you.' I smile. 'Thank you for your help.'

'Michaela told me how you out-foxed Roger.' He blinks at me through his glasses. 'Clever thinking, coming up with that sketchbook.'

My eyes stray to the map on the wall before us, automatically searching for Enysyule.

'Geoff?' I ask, staring at the thickly wooded riverbanks and hillsides. 'Do you know if there were any plane crashes around here, during the Second World War?'

'An interesting question.' He takes off his glasses, starts to polish them on his shirt, as though that will help him see the past more clearly. 'There *was* an airbase, not too far away, and another one, down the coast. Some of the airmen were billeted in the village. But crashes?' He puts his glasses back on. 'Hard to tell. There could have been. The government tended to hush them up, in case it damaged morale.' He raises his eyebrows at me. 'Another mystery you're trying to solve?'

'Something like that.'

'Miss Pike!' someone calls, and I'm accosted by Reg from the village shop, his cheeks rosy, a mince pie balanced on his glass. 'Coming to Montol, arr'ee? I should hope so.'

'I am,' I tell him, cooling my own face on the back of my hand. 'I'll be accompanying Mel actually.'

Reg blinks, mince pie hovering forgotten near his mouth. 'Mel?' he asks incredulously. 'Mel *Roscarrow*?'

'Yes.' I laugh at his surprise. 'We're friends now. Jack said he needed a little encouragement to get out of the house, so we're going together.' I take another sip of the sweet, mulled wine.

'Mel coming to Montol,' Reg murmurs, eyes wide. ''Scuse me, Miss Pike.' He hurries away, into the crowd.

'What was that all about?' I ask Liza, who has appeared, a tray of cheese straws in hand.

'Did I hear you say you're going to Montol with Mel?'

'Yes, how fast exactly does news travel around here?' I reach for a cheese straw.

'What are you going to wear?' she asks, seriously.

'What?' I frown over at her. 'I don't know. Hadn't thought about it. People dress up, right?'

'People dress up?' Michaela has heard us, and bustles over to squeeze in next to me. She's wearing a festive cardigan, a pair of reindeer antlers perched on her coiffed up-do. 'Is the pope a Catholic?' She supresses a burp, and reaches for a cheese straw.

'My grandma used to call what people wear "midjans and jouds".' Liza smiles. 'Shreds and tatters. The whole point of Montol is that things aren't what they seem, poor is rich, darkness is light.'

'You'd better lend her something, Liza,' Michaela says, 'or she'll stick out like a sore thumb in the procession.'

'*Procession*?' I repeat, as Michaela sweeps off towards the mulled wine. 'Jack didn't mention anything about a procession.'

Liza laughs. 'Sorry, Mel's always in the procession. At least, he always was, until he stopped coming a few years ago.

It'll be good to have him back.' She shoots me a sidelong glance. 'I take it that you and Jack have straightened things out, then?'

'Yes, although I'm going to have to give him a piece of my mind after this.' I sip at the mulled wine. 'Do you know if he's ... going with anyone?'

'You mean as a date?' Liza snorts. 'I doubt it. Always says he's too busy at the yard for that sort of thing.'

'Oh.' I try to keep the disappointment from showing on my face.

'Why do you ask?'

'No reason.' I hope she can't tell that I'm blushing. 'So, what time do I have to start *processing* on Saturday?'

'Six o'clock.'

'Until?'

Liza grins and tops up my wine. 'Until we've drunk the old year dry.'

* * *

A thunder of hooves and drums and hearts, a rush of blood through the arteries of the earth. The fire roars. The trees burn green. The sun sets on the shortest day, welcoming the longest night ...

* * *

Saturday takes forever to arrive, and even longer to pass. I spend the morning writing, moving closer and closer to the end of the novel. Another few days, and it should be done. Which is good, because another few days are all I have. My editor has been pretty adamant about having the manuscript by Christmas Eve, so he can take it home to read over the holidays. I wince when I realise how rough it will be, with no time for a proper edit. I'll just have to make my excuses and prepare myself for a barrage of notes in the new year.

Finally, as the hours tick over into afternoon, I can't sit still any more. I shove my laptop to one side and go to organise my costume for the evening. Liza has lent me a dress; ankle-length, bottle-green velvet, with sleeves that fall over my hands. It's a bit too big, but a leather belt around my waist sorts that out. I untangle a bundle of necklaces and bangles from my jewellery box, as instructed by Liza. 'The more the better,' she told me. My hair has got longer, falling to my shoulders now. I pin it up, to get it out of the way, and survey the result doubtfully. All in all, I look a bit like a druid, or someone off to a hippy festival, which, I suppose, is the point.

Outside, night is falling, darkness creeping from the corners of the sky. Time to be going. Despite my reservations, some of Lanford's feverish excitement must have rubbed off on me, because anticipation fills my chest, like moths fluttering against a lamp. *A night where anything can happen . . .*

Perrin isn't in his usual place by the fire. He is sitting on the windowsill, a smudge of dark fur against the night. I call his name and he turns. His eyes are bright as gorse, sharp as an owl's, an ancient creature ready to hunt . . . I blink and the look is gone. It's just Perrin, who meows at me softly and returns to his contemplation of the gathering night.

I hurry through the valley, the sky rapidly shifting from deep blue to black above me. I have to rely on a torch for part of the way, and it's a relief when the loam of the wood gives way onto the rough ground of the yard, the lights from the boathouse spilling welcomingly onto the water's surface.

'Mel?' I call as I let myself in. 'Sorry I'm late, I had to—'

I stop in my tracks. At the top of the stairs is a figure, like something from an old tale. His hair and beard are a mass of twigs, his eyes lost behind a mask of green. On his head, he wears a crown of holly, the berries burning like the low winter sun. A cloak falls from his shoulders, a magnificent, tattered thing of gold and green and red. Then, the regal expression cracks, the mask is pulled away and it's Mel standing there, grinning sheepishly.

'All right, Jessie,' he says.

'Mel!' I blurt, momentarily speechless. 'You look ... amazing!'

'Well, I'm the Holly King,' he says proudly. 'Folks expect a bit of a show. Come on up.'

I follow him upstairs, wishing I'd made more of an effort.

'So, where's Jack?' I ask. The rest of the house is quiet. 'Isn't he coming too?'

'He's already up there,' Mel says. Above his beard, his cheeks have turned a bit pink as he places a box on the table in front of me. 'I had the lad at the florist make this,' he says brusquely, 'in case you had a fancy to wear it. No bother if not, though.'

Curious, I open the lid. The scent of freshly cut evergreen rises out, resin and sap and leaves, just as strong as in my dream. I lift out a crown. Where his is holly, this one is ivy; leaves and branches woven into a spiral, decorated with bare twigs that shimmer as though with frost.

'It's beautiful,' I murmur. 'Of course I'll wear it.'

'Ah, well.' He shuffles with the box, looking pleased. 'You'll be needing a mask too. I've got a spare.'

With the mask obscuring the top of my face and the wreath of ivy on my head, I feel as though I am slipping into another person, not Jessamine Pike, or Jessie or even Jess, instead, a woman made from leaves, with no name at all. Arm in arm, Mel and I make our way to the start of the procession. They're not far away, assembling by the bridge that leads into Lanford, a carpet of lights in the darkness. Torches flame and candle lanterns flicker, fairy lights are wrapped around hats and woven through coats, paper lanterns sway on sticks like huge, ponderous glow-worms.

'Mel,' I whisper, as others start to take their places, 'do I have to do anything?'

He shakes his head. 'Nah. Just walk with me to t'other end of town—'

His words are drowned by a cheer. Instruments burst into life, fiddles and drums and pipes, and then we're moving, as if driven by a will not entirely our own, up the hill and into the crowded village.

Christmas lights banish the darkness, yet at the same time, shadows dance in every corner and crevice. The costumes are exuberant and bewildering; people in bright, tattered cloaks and old-fashioned ball gowns, girls with feathers and ribbons in their hair, men with antlers on their hats, people masked as birds and beasts and otherworldly creatures. All of them squeeze to sides of the street as the procession passes. I peer into the crowd, searching for a familiar face. A woman wearing a feathered mask waves to me, holding a small child by the hand. It's Liza, I realise. I wave back as best I can.

The throng is getting thicker as we pass the Lamb, spilling downhill towards the river. The whole atmosphere is magnetic; I feel myself being pulled into the spirit of Montol, determined to drink this old winter night to its dregs. On the riverbank, a huge bonfire of scrap and driftwood has been assembled, waiting to be lit. I find myself herded around to the far side, with the dark water of the Lan at my back. I search the crowd, but there's still no sign of Jack. Instead, I hear Mel make a gulping noise beside me.

'Are you all right?' I call, over the crowd and the music.

'Aye,' he pats my arm, and I see that his hands are shaking. 'Just reminds me of Phyllis is all. We started courting at Montol, nigh on fifty-one years ago to the day.'

I cover his worn hand with mine. 'She'd be glad to see you here.'

He gives me a sad smile, and a nod. 'You're right at that. Thank you for escorting me, young Jessie.'

A voice booms from the front of the bonfire, and Mel straightens up beside me, growing tall and regal once more.

'Here we go,' he murmurs out of the corner of his mouth, and then he's striding forwards, taking a torch from one of the attendants. He raises it to the sky, and the crowd claps and cheers, before he bends to touch it to the kindling. Within a couple of heartbeats, the flames are climbing like fiery acrobats, leaping from one piece of wood to the next, driving the crowd back a few paces from their heat.

'What now?' I shout to Mel, as we mingle with the crowd.

'Now,' he pats my arm, 'I reckon it's high time you young folk went and enjoyed yourselves.'

He's looking over my shoulder, and I turn to find a man standing behind me. He's in full Montol attire, wearing a waistcoat sewn all over with shreds and patches, a bright red scarf around his neck and a black mask, hiding his eyes. When I hesitate, he raises the mask, revealing a pair of bright hazel eyes that are creased in amusement.

'Jack!' I laugh. 'I didn't recognise you!'

He grins back. 'That's the point.'

I turn to look for Mel, feeling bad about leaving him, but he's already been swallowed up by a group of well-wishers.

'Come on,' Jack bends to murmur in my ear, 'he'll be lording it up in the Lamb in no time.' He catches my hand and pulls me away, into the crowd.

There are stands selling mulled wine, and cider and punch, there's a hog roast, and knots of musicians and dancers. I find myself squeezed around a brazier with Jack and a few of his friends, playing Guess Who with people in the crowd. I see Michaela, dressed like the Master of the Hunt, a foxtail protruding from her coat. Jack spies Liza's cousin Pete, wearing a lurid yellow cocktail dress. We even spot Roger Tremennor, dressed in a black cape and a Venetian mask, surrounded by a few of the people I remember from the Allantide party. Jack puts a hand on my shoulder when his friends point them out, but it doesn't bother me; I'm having too much fun to think about the Tremennors.

One drink becomes three, becomes four. I catch Jack's arm in mine as we weave through the crowd. His hands linger around my waist as he gives me a boost to the top of a post box, so I can watch a performance over the shoulders of the crowd. The night wears on, growing later, and we begin to stand closer, until I can feel the heat of his skin through his cotton shirt, become acutely aware of his lips, so close to mine as he bends to say something in my ear. Whenever we catch eyes, a thousand words and none pass between us, until one of us has to grin or laugh or turn away to break the tension.

The crowd nearby launches into another lively dance, and Jack holds out a hand in invitation. I take it gladly, and for one fleeting instant imagine pulling him away into the shadows, where the Christmas lights don't reach and we can be alone, the alcohol and music thrilling through our veins . . . Then Liza's husband Dan is there, beckoning us in to the dancing throng, and we're swallowed by a mass of whirling bodies. It's a sort of circle dance, and I soon find myself separated from Jack, dancing with a woman I've never seen before, both of us laughing helplessly when we mess up the steps and canter in the wrong direction to everyone else. And although it's a riot, when I feel a hand grasp mine again, pull me urgently away from the crowd, I'm more than happy to follow.

Some of the torches have started to gutter and die, and without their light, the corners of the buildings have been thrown into darkness. *So much the better*, a wicked voice in my head says. I trip on the kerb, and Jack catches me, holds me upright, both of us breathless from dancing. I laugh, telling him about how I completely lost the steps, but he's leaning in, pressing me back against a wall, his body against mine, lips hard and urgent.

For an instant I can't move. I've been dreaming of this moment and yet ... this is all wrong, everything about it makes me want to recoil. I catch a wisp of scent, horribly familiar, and I realise why. Furious, I drag my face away.

'What the hell do you think you're doing?'

Alex stumbles backwards as I shove him, breathing raggedly. He's dressed in a white shirt, a black mask similar to Jack's.

'Jess, please,' he slurs, stepping close again, reaching a hand towards my face.

Just as I'm about to push him once more, I see movement over his shoulder. Jack is standing at the edge of the dancers, mask hanging from his hand. He is staring straight at us. My stomach plummets, even as Alex leans in to try and kiss me again. I push him away, too late. Jack is disappearing into the crowd, hurt etched across his face.

I try to lunge after him, but Alex grabs my hand. 'Jess, please.' Even from arm's length, I can smell the alcohol on his breath. 'You look so beautiful, just give me a chance—'

This time, I put all of my strength into a shove that sends him stumbling backwards, crashing to the floor. I don't waste any more time yelling at him, just push my way into the dancing crowd, into the discordant music and flailing bodies that before were so merry. The notes swirl round me as I fight my way to the other side of the street, but even before I get there, I know that it will be too late.

*　　*　　*

During these dark, December days, the land waits. It waits as the Wild Hunt passes out of hearing, like thunder to the west. It waits as the old year fades, like mist in the sun, the new year not yet born. It waits, as everything hangs in the balance.

★   ★   ★

The morning of December 22nd slides beneath the curtains, waking me with a sore head and an aching heart. For a few heartbeats I lie still, but, all too soon, it comes back to me. Lips on mine, the smell of alcohol, Jack's face, his expression shifting from shock and dismay into hurt as he turns his back ... I bury my head in the pillow. I was so focused on Jack, it never occurred to me that Alex might be at Montol too. I should've looked closer at who took my hand, should've fought harder to catch up with Jack and explain things. Now, in the gap between night and morning everything has calcified, turned brittle and hard to break.

Miserably I shove aside the covers and climb out of bed. My clothes lie in a heap on the floor, where I threw them off last night, in tears. The ivy wreath is there too, withering now, its lustre gone. In the mirror, my face looks pale, eyes puffy from crying, make-up smeared beneath them.

I can't face the day, not yet. Perrin greets me with his usual barrage of breakfast meows, though not so loud or insistent as usual, as if he can tell I need the world to be gentle with me, for a while. Instead of making my usual toast and eating breakfast with him, I shove my feet into boots and head for the bathroom. Although the boiler howls and clanks like there's a poltergeist trapped inside it, whatever Mrs Hesketh did works; the steam rising from the hot tap is almost enough to make me smile. Hurriedly I undress, shivering on the freezing-cold stone floor, and sink into the scalding water before it cools. Fiercely I scrub at my face, at my hair, my skin, trying to wash away the memories of last night, without success.

I should be sitting down to write, trying to hammer out the last few chapters before my Christmas Eve deadline, but I can't. I have to see Jack, I have to tell him what happened, even if that means confessing my feelings for him in the most awkward of circumstances. I set out towards the riverbank, a dozen possible conversations skittering through my head. In the clearing, the stone looks the same as ever, though today there's a sensation of weariness in the air, of heavy eyes lifted from the floor, as if it is waiting for something, or someone, and cannot sleep until they come.

As I approach the boatyard, my empty stomach begins to squirm. Perhaps it will all be fine, I tell myself. Perhaps in ten minutes I'll be sitting at the kitchen table, eating bacon and eggs and laughing this whole thing off. Setting foot after foot, I force myself up to the front door.

There's no answer. They're not asleep still, surely? I'm about to knock again when I hear the sound of footsteps, crunching around the side of the house. My heart shoots into my throat as I stand there waiting.

'Jack—'

Mel comes around the corner carrying an armful of wood. He's squinting in the light, his steps slow and careful. I try to summon up a smile for him.

'You look like I feel,' I call.

He glances up in surprise. 'Jessie.' A frown flickers across his face, to be replaced by a quick smile. He obviously knows something is wrong. 'Cup of tea?'

'Yes please.' I open the door for him. 'Is—' I swallow drily. 'Is Jack here? I need to speak to him.'

''Fraid not,' Mel says, dropping the armful of wood with a groan. 'He left this morning, though I've no notion how he dragged himself out of bed so early.'

'Oh. Do you know when he'll be back? Maybe I could wait.'

Mel shakes his head, a pained smile on his face. 'Not like to be anytime soon. He's gone to pick his sister up from the airport, least that's what his note said.'

I bite the inside of my mouth to stop the tears from welling up, though I can feel them, crowding my chest.

'Something happen betwix you?' Mel asks. 'When Jack left last night he had a face like the back end of a thundercloud. Wudden say anything of it, though.'

I can't keep the tears in any more, and turn away as they spill from my lashes.

'Here,' Mel says, putting an arm about my shoulder. 'Here, there's no call for that. Whatever's amiss it will be put right. Did the pair of you quarrel?'

I nod, swiping at the tears that keep pushing themselves from my eyes. 'It's just a stupid misunderstanding,' I tell him thickly, 'but Jack – he'll think the worst of me until I can explain.'

'Don't fret, Jessie. He'll come round in the end, even if he is a stubborn old weasel.'

That makes me laugh, enough that I can wipe my face on my sleeve and try to smile.

'There now,' Mel says. 'Yuletide's no time for tears. And didn't you say you had company coming to visit?'

'Yes,' I sniff. 'They're getting the train down on Christmas Eve.'

'Well, my guess is you've plenty to do before they arrive,' Mel says practically. 'And no time to waste mopping and moping over my fool grandson.'

'You will let me know,' I ask, 'when he's going to be back?'

'I will,' Mel promises. 'Now, come and have that cup of tea. I've a hangover the size of Devon.'

Mel gives me Jack's number, though I feel awkward asking for it, and I spend the walk back to the cottage trying to compose a text. Before I step into the clearing, I look down at the few words on the screen, the only ones I've been able to come up with.

Jack, I'm sorry. Can we talk? Jess.

They seem pathetic, too thin and paltry to express every-thing I'm feeling. I press send, watch as those seven words of hope disappear into the ether.

Despite Mel's words about it being Yuletide, and a time for happiness, I can't settle down to anything. A few hundred words of writing and I'm pacing the room again, finding excuses to go outside where the signal is better, to see if I've had any reply. Finally, as the afternoon wears into evening, my phone delivers a message, though not the one I want.

Sorry about last night. I was really drunk but that's no excuse for being an idiot. Sorry. Alex. X

It doesn't exactly help my mood. *Tell that to Jack,* I send, before I can stop myself.

Perrin is uneasy too; he stalks about the house as though searching for something, curling in his favourite spots only to leap down again, tail flicking, fur bristling at invisible elec-tricity in the air. By the time darkness falls, we've both worn ourselves out, and slump, staring into the flames.

'This is ridiculous,' I tell him. 'Mel's right, sitting about and brooding isn't going to help.'

With a burst of energy, I throw open the door. Waiting by the step are the armfuls of holly I cut recently from the grove. The branches are damp with night; they fill the cottage with their pungent, green scent, just as they did in my dream. I'll make the cottage festive with holly and deco-rations, and when my family come to visit they'll realise why I love it here so much. We'll sit beside the fire, and I'll tell them everything that's happened. We'll drink and eat, until the room is filled with Christmas scents, orange and spices, saffron and port; and on Christmas Day, Perrin will chase bits of wrapping paper and ribbon about the flagstones, making us all laugh.

Eventually I realise that a tune has joined my drifting thoughts; that I am humming the song I learned from my dreams.

'*Kelynn, kelynn,*' I sing under my breath, placing holly boughs above the fireplace.

One by one, I unpack the decorations from their crate. Perrin watches me work, his head on his paws, as though lost in thought. I discover glass baubles, dented metal shapes and wooden figures – ships and kings and shepherds – their paint faded. I hang them amongst the holly, where they form their own procession through the leaves, while above, tin stars shine down. Last of all, I take up the green glass ornament and hang it in the very centre, where it glimmers like a moon or a sun, or a window to another world.

Christmas Eve dawns, bright and clear and cold. Freezing cold. I open the door to peek outside. The valley looks magical; every branch rimed with frost, glimmering in the pale winter sun. Puddles have iced over in the gaps between the cobbles and every blade of grass is stiff and frozen, as though time itself has been stopped. Perrin comes to my side to sniff at the air, but before long we both retreat to have our breakfast by the warmth of the fire. I look around the cottage, trying not to drop toast crumbs on the clean flagstones. At least my distraction has been good for something. It looks neat and tidy, the hearth swept, the table polished, decorations sparkling in the glow of the crackling fire. Upstairs, beds wait, piled with blankets to huddle beneath after a merry evening. Now all I need are the people to share it with.

The bright sky buoys my mood as I wrap a thick scarf around my neck, shove my laptop into my bag. On the hard drive, an – admittedly rather hasty – manuscript sits waiting to be sent.

'It's Christmas Eve,' I tell Perrin firmly, 'and I'm going to enjoy myself. If Jack Roscarrow is too stubborn to listen to explanations, then it's his loss. Isn't it?'

Perrin doesn't reply, only twitches an ear, waiting patiently by the door for me to get ready. When I leave, he follows me out, though I try to dissuade him. His movements have been slower over the past few days, and I worry that the freezing weather will only make things worse. Of course, he takes no notice, and insists on being my escort all the way to the stone, padding silently alongside me.

It's not like him to be so quiet, and when we reach the clearing I bend down to stroke his ears, to look into his eyes and make sure he's all right. The gaze that meets mine is grave, almost stoic, and for a moment I forget that he's a cat, want to ask this strange, solemn creature what is troubling him.

But he only rubs his head against my palm and sits down, leaving me to make my way across the clearing. When I look back, he's still there; framed perfectly by the hole in the stone, just watching. As absurd as it is, I find myself raising a hand in farewell.

Lanford is busy, children released from school, people off work, relatives visiting for the first day of the holiday. Christmas trees glimmer through windows, wreaths of holly and poinsettia and bright ribbons hang from doors, even some of the boats have been decorated, their masts wound with tinsel.

The café-post-office-bait-shop is heaving with people taking shelter from the bitter cold, their hands wrapped around mugs of hot chocolate. I manage to squeeze onto a table at the back, use the wifi to send the manuscript off to my editor. I tap out a quick message, warning him of how rough it is and wishing him a Merry Christmas. I hit send, and sigh with relief as it disappears.

Despite my resolution to enjoy Christmas, thoughts of Jack keep creeping up on me, and I find myself looking through the steamed-up windows at every person who passes, listening for his laugh amongst the chatter. Eventually

I pull myself together and give up my table to a trio of old ladies. On the way to the village shop, my phone buzzes.

Hey sis, crazy weather here! Train's delayed but we should be on the move soon. X

I look up at the sky doubtfully. Although I hadn't noticed before, the weather is definitely turning, clouds grey as wet wool rolling in to cover the sky. In the shop, people edge past each other down the aisles, shopping for forgotten odds and ends. Luckily I've already got everything I need, delivered to my door yesterday by Reg's nephew on his quad bike.

'Miss Pike.' Reg beams when he sees me, a Christmas elf hat balanced on his bald head. 'Get your delivery OK? You and Perrin haven't eaten it all I hope?'

'No,' I laugh, 'just wanted to say Merry Christmas, Reg.'

'Merry Christmas, Miss Pike. You say you had family coming from London?'

'They're on their way now. At least I hope so. Bad weather up there, apparently.'

A man in a voluminous coat, who I recognise as one of the fishermen, thumps a bottle of sherry down on the counter.

'Aye, it's gluthering up something rotten,' he announces. 'Wouldn't be surprised if it were snow.'

'Snow, in Cornwall?' I snort. 'I'll believe that when I see it.'

'You'll see it tonight, by my reckoning,' the man says, stowing the bottle in one of his pockets. 'Merry Christmas to you, Miss Pike.' He pauses in the doorway. 'And ... to himself.'

By the time I cross the bridge, an icy wind has started up, scudding across the surface of the water. Despite all my best intentions I can't resist taking a detour via the boatyard, even though I know they've probably left for Jack's parents' place already. Sure enough, when I crunch into the yard the place has a locked up feel to it. The mismatched windows, which usually glow so welcomingly, are dark; the workshops and sheds are silent. I knock on the door, just in case, but there's no answer.

A little sadly, I make my way into the woods, back towards Enysyule. As I walk, the afternoon light is being swallowed into the sky, flushing darker and darker, even though night is still hours away. The air feels thick in my lungs, like breathing crushed ice. As I step into the clearing, all sound vanishes, as though it's been sucked from the world, and I see that the old fisherman was right.

Softly, almost imperceptibly, snow has started to fall, spiralling into the circle of bare ground, onto the Perranstone. I watch the first few flakes land, motes of pure white against the ancient, gnarled surface. I turn my face to the mouth of the sky, letting the snow brush my cheeks, my eyes, melt against the heat of my skin. As it does, I swear I hear voices, drifting past my ears, at the very edge of hearing.

And although the words are indistinct, although some are whispered and some are shouted and some cried or sung, I know they belong to this valley; I know that Enysyule has taken these voices and is giving them back to me as echoes, now, centuries later.

Hands carve stone, feet run, hooves canter, lips part to sing, tears fall on snow, and through everything that has happened, there is a presence; one that is always the same. Old eyes, yellow eyes, wild as a hawk's. I thought it was a trick of my imagination, seeing him in all of my dreams, but what if it wasn't? What if he *has* always been here, watching, protecting? And yet ... I open my eyes. Tonight is no ordinary night. It is Christmas Eve. The very heart of Yule; the burning coal at the centre of the blaze. A night when people once believed that the walls between the worlds were thin and spirits walked the earth.

Abruptly I remember Perrin's odd, grave manner this morning, the way he sat in the clearing and watched me leave, like a soul who knows his time is approaching, and must wait to meet it. The stone behind me is waiting too. Against the falling snow, it looks larger than before. It looms in the clearing, deep grey against the speckled white ground, impatient for this Yule night to begin.

Foreboding floods my mind.

'Perrin,' I whisper, and take off towards the cottage at a run.

★   ★   ★

Where there is flint, there will again be flame. Where there is fuel, there will once more be fire. Wherever there are humans, there will always be hope. And hope – the Land knows – makes for the best kind of kindling …

★   ★   ★

By the time I reach the front door, winded and with a stitch in my side, the falling snow has started to settle, collecting on top of the garden wall, making the thatch of the cottage look as though it has been dusted with flour. I let myself in and shove the door closed behind me. Everything looks as it did when I left that morning.

'Perrin!' I call. There's no reply, no chirrup of greeting or meow of indignation. The armchair by the hearth is empty. I place my hand against the cushion, but the fabric there is cold.

I call his name again and stand still, listening, expecting to hear the sound of paws hitting the wooden floor above me, scampering down the stairs. I check all his favourite sleeping places; the windowsills, the rug, but he's nowhere to be seen. I even run outside to check the bathroom, just in case he's got shut in there.

'Perrin?' I shout out the front door, banging a tin of tuna, a trick that usually never fails. There's no movement, nothing except the snow, falling swift and silent across the valley. I shut the door again, my mind reeling, leaping to all of the worst possible conclusions.

The bedrooms, I tell myself, trying to calm down, *go and double-check the bedrooms, maybe he's asleep and hasn't heard you.*

I run up the stairs two at a time, making them creak and moan, and barge into the spare room. It's undisturbed, the beds neatly made up and ready, the windowsill empty. I fling myself around the corner into my room, only to slam my shin against the trunk at the end of the bed.

'Shit,' I swear. He's not here, not on the bed, not on the pile of clothes in one corner. Tears spring to my eyes that have nothing to do with the pain in my leg. *He'll be back,* I think desperately, *any minute now he'll scratch at the door or clatter in through the pantry window.* And yet there's no ignoring the anxiety gnawing at my gut, the inexplicable certainty that something is wrong.

The trunk is askew from where I kicked it. I push it back into place, hand lingering over the many scratches in the wood, where Perrin must have sharpened his claws again and again over the years. My finger catches on something there, protruding half an inch from the side. I bend to look: a cube of wood, darkened by time, blending in perfectly with the trunk around it. I wiggle it free. It slides out, tapering to a point, like a stake for securing something closed. I stare at it, heart beating faster. I've been looking for a key to open the trunk, but what if there is no key? What if, like everything else at Ensysyule, the trunk keeps its secrets in a different way?

Swiftly I grope around the other side of the trunk. Sure enough, I feel the same thing there, a cube, protruding just enough to grasp with my fingertips. It falls to the floor with a clatter. The trunk's knot-eyes gaze at me in the dying light, as, half-hypnotised, I place my hands on the lid, and lift it open.

Colours rise from the gloom, threads of green and ochre and grey, stitched onto what looks like a quilt, folded carefully in the bottom of the trunk. On top of it is something that makes me catch my breath; an envelope, thick, creamy paper, addressed with just two words:

Dear Stranger

My hands move as though they're not my own, lifting the letter, breaking the seal on the back of the envelope without a second thought. Inside is a single sheet of writing paper, filled with familiar handwriting, and a date, Christmas Eve, one year ago.

Dear Stranger,

I hope that was as fun for you to read as it was for me to write! If you're reading this, then I suppose I'm dead. (If I'm not *dead and you're not a stranger, but my nephew Melvin or Mrs Welwyn from the village poking around then STOP READING AT ONCE AND PUT THIS BACK. It isn't meant for you.)*

It's meant for you, stranger. I hope by now you have begun to discover the joys of this valley, my beloved Enysyule. I say 'begun', because I've lived here my entire life, and still I don't know all its secrets. Sometimes, weeks will pass without one. Then, my eye will catch upon a spark of dew in the meadow, or my ear will be hooked by the call of a crow, or from nowhere, my nose will be filled with the scent of saffron and rain, and I will disappear, for a while. When I return, I'll know a little more than I did before about this place. I don't know if it will be the same for you, but I'm sure the valley will find a way to make itself heard. It always has, in the past.

Most importantly, by now, you will have met himself. If you're reading this at all, you must have met with his approval, or I imagine you wouldn't have lasted much more than a night here. Perrin is a good judge of character, you'll find, and I trust him to decide whether or not you will be

*right for this place. I trust too that you will look after him,
just as I did, and my mother before me, and my father's
family before her.*

*This will be my last Yuletide at Enysyule, stranger. I can
feel it. And so, once this old year is done, and the new has
taken its first steps, I will make my preparations. You, I hope,
will be the result; someone to care for this valley the way I
have, someone to care for Perrin, to remind him of home and
hearth, see that he does not turn wild. Someone with new eyes
and a new name: one that is not tangled in half a millennium
of bitterness and grudges. I had hoped to bring another name
to this place, had hoped to have children who would bear that
name, their blood a mingling of here and faraway. It was not
to be. And so, stranger, I leave that task to you.*

*I don't know when you will read this; whether there will be
summer sunlight through the cottage windows, or rain on the
thatch, or frost on the ground, but I will wish you a Merry
Christmas, if only because it is my last chance to do so. Save
it for Christmas night, if you wish. I have no doubt you will
learn, if you haven't already, what an extraordinary time of
year this is in the valley. Do not be afraid. Keep the Yule with
my blessings, and watch over Perrin, as he has watched over
me, and will, I hope, watch over you for many years to come.*

Your absent friend,
Thomasina Roscarrow

I stare at the words on the page, hearing Thomasina's voice
in their rhythm. I imagine her flexing her knotted fingers at
the end of each sentence, sitting at the kitchen table, wondering who would be reading her letter, what colour eyes, what
temperament, what name . . . I grip the paper, reading it over
and again, wishing I could write back to her, wishing I could
whisper into the past, tell her that I am here, that I
understand.

Eventually pins and needles in my legs bring me back to myself. I blink rapidly, looking up from the paper, trying to focus on the room around me. The light from the window is dim, mottled and purple as a bruise. It can't be getting dark already, can it?

I scrabble in my pocket for my phone. It feels odd, clumsy and slippery in my hand after the smooth, dry paper. I stare at it in horror; an hour has passed, while I've sat here reading. A whole hour, while outside the snow still falls, and the light is fading and Perrin isn't home. What's more, there are messages on my phone, missed calls. It must have picked up some signal, rung and rung in my pocket without me even feeling it.

Words scroll past my eyes: *delayed, rail replacement, cancelled.* Praying that the signal will hold, I dash to the window and press the call button. My sister answers almost immediately.

'Where have you been?' she demands, voice crackling with the distance. 'I've been calling and calling you!'

'I'm sorry, I only just saw … what's the matter? What's going on?'

'We're stuck,' she says. She sounds fraught. 'The train's been stopped, somewhere in the middle of nowhere, outside Swindon. The snow's messed everything up, Jess—'

'Ana, calm down. Is Mum there?'

I hear a shuffling, the phone being passed from hand to hand, before my mum answers.

'Jessamine, at last, we were starting to get worried.' The sound of her voice is so familiar I want to cry. I wish I could reach out across the miles between us and hug her.

'I'm sorry,' I say instead, 'what's happening?'

On the other end of the phone, I hear her sigh heavily. 'It's the trains, Jessamine, the snow has brought everything to a stop. We haven't moved for an hour now. The driver said they can perhaps get us back to London tonight, but no further.' My mother's voice cracks. 'Darling, I am so sorry, we should have left sooner.'

'No, Mama.' I try to sound calm and controlled, for her sake. 'This isn't your fault. It's the stupid weather. I bet people aren't wishing for a white Christmas now.'

She laughs at that, and I hear her sniffing, blowing her nose.

'Get back to London safely,' I tell her. 'Maybe you can try to catch a train on Boxing Day, they should have the tracks clear by then.'

'But what will you do?' She sounds devastated. 'You can't be on your own, at Christmas.'

'I'm not on my own.' I try to sound cheerful, even though worry is squeezing my chest. 'I've got Perrin, remember? He'll keep me company tomorrow.'

'I mean *human* company, Jessamine. What about your new friends, with the boats? Could you go to them?'

'Yes,' I lie, not wanting to make her feel any worse. 'I'll be fine, I promise. And the turkey will keep for a day or two.'

She says something else, but the signal is fading. I lean into the cold glass, pressing the phone to my ear, trying to keep hold of her voice.

'Mama, I love you, please don't worry.'

'Love you too—' Her voice cuts off into silence, and the phone bleeps, signal gone.

I don't know how long I stand there, the handset still pressed to my ear. I thought this Christmas would be different, would be the start of a new life, shared with the people I love most. None of them are here. Not my mum, not my sister, not my dad, gone for so long . . . not even Perrin.

Watch over him, as he has watched over me.

My eyes stray to the window. It's fully dark outside now. I can see snow, swirling in the light from the bedroom window. I can hear the wind, driving against the cottage. There's no way Perrin would stay outside in this. I only have one choice.

By the front door I pull on my coat, cram my feet into boots, searching frantically for a torch. I find one by the dresser and yank open the door, ready to plunge headfirst into the night.

A dark shape blocks the way, a blot of shadow against the snow. A cry of surprise almost escapes me before a hood is pushed back, light falling across bright hazel eyes, skin that is pink with cold.

'Jess,' Jack says, 'I—'

I throw my arms around his shoulders. I can't help it, not after everything that's happened. For one, endless moment he stands still; then his arms tighten around me, and – almost instinctively – our lips meet. I feel a rush of joy as he kisses me back, his hands moving up to my neck, my face, fingers tangling in my hair. I don't care that his coat is wet and cold with snow, because my body feels like it's burning in all the places that we touch, as we find each other's lips again and again. Finally I have to pull away, bury my face in his shoulder.

'I'm sorry, Jess,' I hear him murmur breathlessly, 'I've been such an idiot. When I saw you with Alex, I just—'

'There's nothing going on between us,' I manage, looking up at him. 'Not any more.'

'I know.' Jack gives a pained sort of laugh and smoothes a strand of hair away from my cheek. 'He sent me a message, weirdly, explained what happened, said he didn't want you to be miserable at Christmas. I drove over here as soon as I got it.' He looks into my eyes. 'I'm sorry. I should have come over days ago.'

He leans in to kiss me again. This kiss is longer, lingering, and I want to lose myself in it, but it's no good: the letter, my family, the joy and relief at seeing Jack, my worry about Perrin are all too much. I feel tears welling up, jolting my chest. Jack pulls away.

'What is it?' he asks, concern creasing his face. 'Jess, what's wrong?'

'I'm sorry.' I wipe my eyes on my sleeve. 'It's . . . Perrin. I can't find him anywhere. Something's happened, I know it.' I wait for him to tell me not to worry, that Perrin will be fine. Instead, I see some of the colour leave his cheeks.

'Perrin's missing?' he says.

'Yes.' I grab at his arm. 'Why? Do you know something?'

'Nothing,' he shakes his head. 'Just old stories.'

'I have to go and look for him.' I step towards the door, expecting him to stop me. He doesn't, only pulls his hood back up over his head.

'It's horrible out there,' he says. 'I'll come with you.'

Together, we stride into the darkness, the snow-filled wind battering our coats, blasting into our faces until my eyes sting. I keep my torch ahead, while Jack scans the ground.

'Perrin!' I yell into the night, over and again. Jack takes over whenever the cold makes my throat seize up, whistling and calling, both of us straining our ears over the storm for any reply. After what feels like an age, we reach the ford. It is freezing over, ice creeping from the edges of the bank. Still no sign. We press on. As the path begins to drop down towards the holly grove a flash of clarity fills my mind, a premonition, and I swear beneath my breath at the inevitability of it all . . . I break into a run, stumbling on hidden tree roots, blinded by snow, barely able to see in the swaying torchlight against the blackness. I hear Jack call my name, but I don't stop.

Holly trees loom out of the darkness without warning. I stagger to a halt between them, gasping, scanning the ground with the torch desperately. It catches on a faint imprint in the snow, the shape of a paw, then another . . . I follow the trail, already knowing where they will lead.

At the foot of the stone, a small black shape is lying in the snow. I drop the torch, stumbling forwards.

'Perrin!' I kneel beside him on the cold, hard ground. The snow has started to collect on his fur. I brush it away from his little face, his ears, expecting him to stir, to make his usual chirrup of greeting. But his eyes are closed, his body still; no breath moves his chest no matter how much I search for it. His paws hang limply when I scoop him up, as I cradle him to my chest, trying to share my warmth, even though I realise it's already too late.

He's gone.

★　　★　　★

In the deepest depths of the Yuletide night, boundaries begin to blur, fading one into another; midnight seeps into morning, land into memory, stone into spirit. Old and new come together in the burning of the hearth, and time is now and was and will be all at once. Yet more remarkable than any of this – as fleeting and fragile as a wave upon the strand – is the human heart, which is vast enough to encompass it all.

★　　★　　★

I barely remember Jack pulling me to my feet, wrapping his arm around my shoulders, keeping me upright on the long walk back towards the cottage. Once there, he makes me let go of Perrin, taking him gently from my arms, wrapping him in a blanket, like he was asleep, and placing him on the pantry floor, near his food dishes. My mind feels like it has become detached from my body, and doesn't find its way back until I feel a blanket settle around me. I look up to see Jack, his face creased in worry.

'You should get home,' I tell him woodenly. 'It's Christmas Eve. Your family will be missing you.'

He smiles wryly. 'I don't think so. I've been pretty bad company for the past few days.' He sits down beside me. 'Where are yours?' he asks. 'I thought they were supposed to be here?'

'They can't come.' I let my head fall back against the chair, and close my eyes. 'The trains were cancelled, because of the snow.'

After a while, I hear movement and look up to find Jack unlacing his boots.

'What are you doing?' I hear myself say.

He peels off a sodden sock. 'I'm not going to leave you on your own, on Christmas Eve, am I? Besides, it's snowing too much to drive.'

My eyes fill with tears. 'You don't have to.'

He leans over, kisses me, his hand warm on my cheek. 'I'm staying, Jess,' he says simply.

Upstairs, I pull on a dry jumper and trousers. The trunk still stands open, Thomasina's letter on the bed where I left it. I reach into the trunk, pull out the quilt that's folded there. It's heavy and cool, smells of cedar. I take both downstairs.

'I found these earlier,' I tell Jack quietly, handing over the letter. 'In the trunk at the foot of the bed. I was never able to open it, before.'

Jack's eyes scan the words, before his gaze falls on the quilt in my arms.

'I've seen this,' he murmurs, 'once before, when I was a kid. It was summer, my parents were away and Amy was at a friend's house. I was staying at the yard, but then Grandpa had to take Grandma Phyllis to the hospital and there was no one else to look after me.' He takes it from my arms. 'So I came here. Thomasina made up a bed for me, and I slept under this . . .' He shakes it out, spreading it flat on the thread-bare rug.

I've never seen anything like it. It's beautiful, made from scraps and patches of fabric in different shades, all of them the colours of Enysyule; grey, green, ochre. Stone-coloured satin, linen like the sky above the clearing on a winter's day. Old gold brocade like the filigree of lichen on the thatch. Green in a dozen shades, cool and slippery as riverweed, startlingly bright as new leaves, sumptuous and thick as holly. The patches fan out from the very centre of the quilt, where pieces of black velvet have been sewn into curves and arches, two, gorse-yellow circles embroidered in the middle. It's impossible to deny what – who – the shape is meant to be.

I stroke the fabric, soft as the fur of Perrin's ears. It brings tears to my eyes all over again, for Thomasina, for Perrin, for everything that could have been. Jack sits down and pulls me close, wrapping his arms around me. In happier times, my heart would have sung to see us like this. Now, any joy I feel struggles against sorrow.

'I'll have to leave Enysyule,' I whisper, my head on his shoulder. 'The agreement Thomasina wrote, it's only valid so long as Perrin . . .' I can't go on, just hold him tighter.

'It'll be all right,' Jack whispers, lips against my hair. 'I promise, Jess. Everything will be all right.'

He pulls the quilt over the pair of us. Enysyule's colours gleam in the firelight, reminding me of the first day I ever set foot in the valley. It must be the emotion, the warmth of the fire after the snow, because I feel myself drifting into sleep, propped against the armchair, enfolded in Jack's arms.

★   ★   ★

Holly boughs fill the cottage with the scent of winter trees. A green glass ornament spins gently in the draught from the chimney. The two young people sleep, wrapped in another woman's dream. Unseen to them, the riders of the wild hunt rein in their weary mounts, their quarry stands from where it has fallen, and leaps away, disappearing in an eddy of snow as – between one breath and another – Christmas night slips into Christmas morning . . .

★   ★   ★

My legs have gone to sleep. So has one of my arms, not to mention the crick in my neck. I groan and stretch, only to find my legs tangled with someone else's. I look up blearily to see Jack rubbing his eyes.

He smiles down at me drowsily, his dark hair in disarray. 'I can't feel my legs,' he mumbles.

'Me neither.'

He laughs, shifting his weight, pulling the quilt higher around us. I let my head fall back against his shoulder, feel him lean to kiss my hair. What was it that woke me up? A noise, I think sleepily, a quiet noise, a sort of scuffling. *Mice?* I wonder. *I've never heard mice before.* Just as I drift into a doze, it starts up again, scratching, scrabbling, accompanied by a mournful cry . . . I sit bolt upright, the night rushing back to me.

'Perrin!'

'Jess!' Jack reaches for me as I untangle myself from the quilt. 'Jess, wait—'

There's no waiting. Ignoring the numbness in my legs, I lurch across the room, and throw open the front door. Daylight floods in, blinding me. Snow has covered the valley; the trees, the meadow, even the path has disappeared beneath a layer of white, perfect and undisturbed. Except for one, tiny line of prints, leading up out of the wood, all the way to the doorstep.

Not daring to breathe, I look down. Eyes look back at me, yellow as tallow, yellow as corn, wild as a hawk's . . . *Feet running through the valley, snow and the sun, dawn and dusk, a stone that has stood for thousands of winters, will stand for thousands more.*

The kitten mews indignantly and I'm bending down to gather it into my arms, burying my face in its cold, soft fur as

I've done so many times in the past. It squeaks, little claws gripping the wool of my jumper. It is big for a kitten, with fur as black as coal. It looks over my shoulder and mews again, and I turn to find Jack standing in the doorway of the pantry, the blanket he used to wrap Perrin hanging empty in his hand.

'Jess,' he says urgently. Then his eyes find the kitten, its cold paws busily kneading my sleeve, and his mouth falls open.

I can't say anything, crying with happiness, can only laugh as he comes forward, raising a tentative hand towards the kitten's head. It eyes him solemnly, before headbutting his palm.

'I knew it,' he whispers.

'Knew what?' I'm finally able to ask.

'Nothing,' he says, face breaking into a grin. 'Just old stories.'

We take the kitten over to the fireplace and place him on the quilt, staring in wonder as he sniffs the black cat figure sewn there, before scrambling up onto the armchair. After turning a few circles, he settles down, a tiny, black proprietorial lump, as though he has always been there.

'What do we call him?' I murmur, mind a blur.

'I think he already has a name. I think he's always had one.'

'Stone and spirit,' I whisper, and the kitten glances up at me.

'What's that?' asks Jack.

'Nothing.' The smile grows on my face as I look over at him, reach for his hand. 'Just dreams.' He smiles back, pulls me in towards him. We're soon interrupted by a long, demanding *meow*.

A few minutes later finds the three of us cosy by the fire once more, Jack and I wrapped in the quilt, mugs of hot chocolate steaming beside us. I breathe in deeply, the cottage filled with the scent of spice and green branches and snow. Perrin sits on the hearth, happily attacking a piece of Christmas salmon.

I raise my mug. 'Merry Christmas, Jack.'

He raises his too, hazel eyes bright with a smile. 'Merry Christmas, Jess. What are we drinking to?'

I look around the cottage, at the worn flagstones and the beams, the fireplace and the weathered table, at the holly boughs around the windows, and the valley outside, guarded by stone.

'To Enysyule,' I tell him.

'To Roscarrow and Tremennor,' Jack grins mischievously, 'and Pike.'

'To the Perranstone.'

'To the Yuletide.'

'To Perrin,' I say and clink my mug with his, 'because there has always been a cat at Yule Cottage.'

And there always will be.

Acknowledgements

This book owes a lot to some of the truly amazing resources that are available online. Among these, I have to thank the Internet Archive for their continued commitment to making historical texts easily accessible, such as Richard Carew's fascinating 1602 text *A Survey of Cornwall*. Cornwall Council's Archives and Cornish Studies Service also provided invaluable information on historical disputes and land registry, whilst An Daras: The Cornish Folk Arts Project provided much needed historical culture and colour! Special thanks go to Merv Davey for allowing me to use a line from his Cornish translation of 'An Ula'. Thanks to my agent, and to the whole team at Hodder for their sterling work whipping this book into publication shape. To my family, for lending an ear during the book's early teething problems, and for reading messy first drafts. To my partner, for coming with me on many Cornish adventures. And of course, thank you to my feline friends: for waking me up in the middle of the night, for trying to sit on my computer, for keeping me company, and for generally making the world that little bit better.